Lillian in Love

by Sue Katz

Published by Consenting Adult Press
Arlington, MA 02474
Copyright 2017 by Sue Katz
All rights reserved
ISBN: 978-0-9913122-4-5

consentingadultpress@hotmail.com

ACKNOWLEDGEMENTS

The splendid British writer **Elizabeth Woodcraft** and I used the framework and tools of the 2015 November National Novel Writing Month to rush out the bones of our books. Because of the UK/USA time difference, she set the bar high by daily overachieving before I even woke up.

The author and innovative sexologist **Gina Ogden** did close readings of both early and late versions and pushed me, as always, to be a better, deeper writer.

Special thanks to **Deborah Bernard** who produced an elegant cover that melds the technical and aesthetic demands of publication. Her heart is as big as her talents.

Thanks to my first editor, **Barry Hock**, who ferrets out every inconsistency, imprecision, and lack of continuity in all of my texts.

Thanks to **Sandy Oppenheimer** for the exquisite cover image, a paper collage portrait of her late mother, **Florence Oppenheimer**. Thanks, too, to **John Fisher**, sculptor extraordinaire, and to **Judy Schwartz**, who helped develop the cover idea. You'll find the story of this cover at the back of this book.

Thanks to **Sue O'Sullivan** for being my rock.

Thanks to my other generous readers in the order of their feedback:

Jaya Schuerch

Verandah Porche

Tracy Moore

Gilbert Ruff

Susan Bonthron

Patricia Gilbert

Marni Warner

Richard Schweid

Thanks to my copy-editor, **Barbara Mende,** for extricating typos and other deviant errors.

Thanks to **Janet Reasoner** for technical and formatting assistance.

Thanks to **Cal Sharp** of Caligraphics for swift formatting and internal design:
www.caligraphics.net

WHAT OTHERS ARE SAYING ABOUT
Lillian in Love

I started reading *Lillian in Love* this afternoon. It's now 7:00pm. What a lovely day it has been. I couldn't stop reading except to pee and smoke a joint. At 86, maybe I'll fall in love, like Lillian, just one last time.

--Betty Dodson, artist, author, and PhD sexologist

Humor, good sex, enticing characters, familial drama – this 76-year-old reader enjoyed it all. Katz breaks new ground with verve, compassion, and sensuality.

--Joan Nestle, archivist, activist, and award-winning author, including *A Fragile Union*

In this era of insult and repression, we all need a good read with a happy ending. Settle on the sofa and pick up *Lillian in Love* now. This is less a coming-out story than a letting-go of the obstacles to the full expression of our being.

--Verandah Porche, poet and performer, whose books include *Sudden Eden*, *Glancing Off*, and *The Body's Symmetry*

Timely and important, this is a novel not to be missed. A great read.

--Elizabeth Woodcraft, author of *Beyond the Beehive* and *A Sense of Occasion*

If you worry that sex has an expiration date, you'll be reassured and inspired by *Lillian in Love*. Katz doesn't sugarcoat the hard realities of the characters' present and past. Fortunately, she also doesn't skip the good parts!

--Joan Price, senior sex advocate and author of *The Ultimate Guide to Sex After 50: How to Maintain – or Regain! – a Spicy, Satisfying Sex Life*

It's a really delightful read, and not just for those of us pushing old age. Sue Katz is a terrific writer and here she's at the top of her game.

--Richard Schweid, journalist and author, most recently of *Invisible Nation: Homeless Families in America*

ABOUT THE AUTHOR

Sue Katz's business card identifies her as a "wordsmith and rebel." She has lived and worked on three continents: first as a martial arts master, then promoting transnational volunteering, and most recently, teaching fitness and dance to seniors and elders. In all her locations, she has been an activist for social justice. Her fiction and non-fiction have been published for decades in anthologies, magazines, and online. Her previous books include *Lillian's Last Affair and other stories* and *Thanks But No Thanks: The Voter's Guide To Sarah Palin.*

You can reach Katz at consentingadultpress@hotmail.com.

WHY I WROTE THIS BOOK

The first story in my collection *Lillian's Last Affair* is a story by that name. That story ends as Lillian and Sarah walk hand-in-hand into Manor House senior housing. Many readers wanted to know what then happened between Lillian and Sarah. Did they get it on? How did Lillian deal with her family's objections to her living at Manor House? Did the other seniors in Manor House accept their relationship? How do two old women negotiate new love? I wrote *Lillian in Love* to find out.

Chapters

Lillian in Love

To be fond of dancing was a certain step
towards falling in love.
— Jane Austen, *Pride and Prejudice*, Chapter 3

1. Two Bras

"Wearing two bras? I'm losing the plot!" I tell Freda. "Packing and moving is so discombobulating. You won't believe what just happened. I'm out of the shower and looking everywhere for my damned black bra. Not on the bed with my other clothes. Not in the suitcase. So I take out my white bra and put that on. Then I pull my sweater over my head, but something's wrong. What's that? The black bra is already around my waist."

"Oy!" says Freda, speaking from her cousin's place in Florida, "Vat a story. I'm laughing me right to the door. I'm going out now, but I'm suggesting to you that you consecrate on finishing the packing and get over to mine place."

As usual, I instantly translate her malapropism. Concentrate! Freda's unrequited love for English is only one of the reasons people adore her. And she's right. How much do I need for my move into Freda's apartment for six weeks, after all? My clothes and books, shoes and slippers, cosmetics and medications bag, and CDs and laptop. To help me feel at home, I pack a half-dozen teas in my favorite decorative basket. On top I carefully lay the present I bought for Sarah more than a week ago. Like a giggly kid, I've already wrapped it in shiny paper and adorned it with some glitter I "borrowed" from Lisa's art box.

Michael spent the morning in selfish pouting. He hasn't even offered me a ride to Manor House from my own home – the one that he and his family of five have colonized. Of late, whenever my son doesn't want to do something, he claims to have a "networking meeting." Unemployment has become his ticket to "de-Nile" – his badge of avoidance. This being that I somehow birthed and raised just can't cope with any more bad news. It's a damn shame that our needs are in conflict. I want to chase this unexpected chance for a last love affair and he wants me to babysit the grandchildren. It's a no-brainer, as they say. I feel for him, I do, but at 84 I don't have time to wheedle his clenched feelings out of him. I'm in a rush toward romance.

The truth? A taxi will be a more peaceful way to get there. If I ride with Michael, he might moan from door to door. I understand his fears about his jobless future – but not today, thank you very much. Today I want to think about the changes that are about to shake up my own life. Before I go, I stop to squeeze some lemon into a tall glass of water and drink it down. I'm parched. The taxi driver honks outside – even though I told the company I'll need help with my bags. I open the door to signal him, but he's already climbing my steep front steps.

Poor Michael. I know my boy. He is sulking upstairs, torn between a goodbye kiss and making a point about my abandoning him. In other circumstances, I'd try to cajole him. But not this time. I'm concentrating on the cliff I'm about to jump off of.

Anticipation speeds up the ride. From the moment I arrive at Manor House Independent Living and the driver unloads my suitcases, I feel pampered. A couple of staff members are there to greet me. Good marketing? After all, they know I'm a potential resident, not just a six-week guest. The guy who actually takes me up to Freda's place, Emmanuel, seems especially warm. And considerate. He checks the inside of the taxi for me and finds the ziplock bag of food I prepared for myself at home, but forgot on the floor of the cab. Emmanuel is tall and slim, but slings my bags around as if they were as light as meringue. He tells me he was just hired a week or so ago. "We will be learning the ways of the Manor House together," he whispers to me in the elevator.

It's good to have a bit of reassurance because frankly, with Freda and Lenny away, I'm on my own. Of course I have Sarah. Well, I hope I do. Or at least I hope I will. That's the whole point of my staying at Freda's while she and Lenny visit their cousins in Florida. To figure out with Sarah how we're going to fit into each other's futures. But since at 84 my future is likely to be short, we've got to shake a tail feather. Or as my granddaughter would say, we need to haul ass.

Before meeting Sarah, I never dreamed of a last affair, but now I've been in a continual state of arousal. Back at my house I've been self-medicating with a suggestive email correspondence with Sarah, and with secret cupcakes, shamefully hidden from my grandchildren in a box in my closet.

All week I've been drawing some boundaries for myself. Like I told Freda when we came up with this plan, "I don't intend to call on Sarah for help every time I have a question about Manor House or need a hand. Just because she's five years younger than me doesn't mean I'm going to be dependent. I want Sarah as my lover, not my caregiver."

"I understand," Freda said. "You only vant her to tuck you in bed if she's in it as vell."

"I will return in a couple of hours when you're unpacked," Emmanuel says, startling me out of my daydream. "There is no room for suitcases in here but we have a place in the basement for storage." I chalk up the idea of storage space that someone else arranges for me as another benefit of Manor House.

Later, when he comes back, he notices the colorful, tightly woven basket full of teas that I've set up on the tiny kitchen counter.

"From where did you get this lovely basket?" he asks.

"It was on my second trip to Kenya, in 1995," I answer. "At a crafts fair outside of Nairobi, I think."

"And did you like my home country?"

"Oh Emmanuel, you're from Kenya! I adore the place. And the people."

Emmanuel's posture relaxes. "I am relieved to find someone at Manor House who mentions my country. Or rather, mentions it with affection."

"Have people here been rude?"

"Not on purpose. But Americans are odd about other places. Some residents have asked me, 'Where are you from?' But when I answer Kenya, the conversations end. When I said I was from Kenya to one gentleman, he twisted up his face as if he had never heard that name and said, 'Africa or something, right?' I answered, 'Yes, something.' The worst was the lady who commiserated with me. 'You must be thrilled to be out of that terrible place and living here in America!'"

I will quickly come to understand that it's only Emmanuel's empathetic approach to the residents that keeps him kind and civil in this job. Despite his degree in architecture from the University of Nairobi, this is the only job he has found. He is making the minimum wage in Manor House, serving elders who each have more wealth than a dozen Kenyan families.

We start to become friends in our own little way. My anecdotes about being a tourist in Kenya are an antidote to his homesickness. And since I don't know anyone else who has visited Kenya, it's a treat for me as well. And to think that I still remember three words of Swahili: *jambo, asante,* and the word for elephant, *tembo.* Who can forget the elephants, their loyalty to each other, their sophisticated relationships. I can still picture the animals I saw from the open jeep – the rhino, the lions, the hippos, even the horrid hyenas who kept us up at night by throwing themselves against the electrified fence around the tent resort.

"My friends Freda and Lenny – you haven't met them; this is Freda's apartment – bought me a little camera. And said I no longer had an excuse. You see, I always said I wanted to go on a wild animal photo safari to Kenya," I explain. "I'm no photographer and I'm not even all that taken with animals, but I'll never forget the 360° view of the sky."

"Where did you stay on your safari?" Emmanuel asks.

"A fancy tent camp in Masai Mara. I stayed there for a week and drove out twice a day. The size of the migrations! I'd sit in that open Jeep and watch the waves of gazelles and zebras – and those rather ugly wildebeests – run towards Zimbabwe."

Emmanuel smiles, mumbles something affirmative, although he is looking at the door. Even though deep down I know I'm holding him up, I keep talking.

"I'll tell you about my surprise at eating zebra

stew one night…"

"Which reminds me," Emmanuel interrupts, "you ought to go downstairs before the dinner is ending."

As I open the door to let him out, Sarah is standing there. Emmanuel passes her with a smile and she slips inside. Before I can even shut the door, she starts talking. "Just came to give you a welcome hug and tell you that dinner is served from 5:00 to 7:00. But I have to warn you about something." I can hardly grasp her rush of words because this is the moment we've been waiting for. Here we are, Sarah and I, starting the gift from Freda of six weeks in which the two of us… well, in which we decide whether or not to get it on. But instead she is talking about mundane things. What an anticlimax.

Before I can finish my thought, she envelops me in a hug, her cheek against mine, her body pressed against me. The hug comes so suddenly that I almost lose my balance. But she holds me up and squeezes even more firmly. When she releases me, she cups my chin in her hand, gazes at me, and then lowers her lips to mine. I exhale with relief. "I needed that," I say.

"That's all for now," she answers. "See you downstairs. Oh, the thing I wanted to say is that I can't sit with you because I've been eating dinner with the same group of friends for over a year – there are four of us and our table's full." She runs off, leaving me nonplused.

2. The Complications of Sitting Down in Senior Housing

Learning last night about Sarah's permanent dinner party was only the first step in my education about the politics of parking my butt, as Bernard used to say. Tonight, though, I get a sharp shove along the steep but crucial learning curve about senior seating.

The elevators and the lobby have been plastered with leaflets about Film Night, so I make my way to the screening room to see "A Streetcar Named Desire." I'm early because I want to be sure to get an aisle seat where I can stretch out my bad leg. It's hard to sit in a cramped position with neuropathy. I twist to watch the door in case Sarah turns up. A tiny woman strides down the side aisle and raps on the back of my seat with her knuckles. "Out!" she rasps, "Out of my seat."

Startled, I struggle up. "Oh, so sorry, I didn't realize you had saved this seat."

"I don't have to save what's mine."

I squeeze out past her, holding my cane aside, even as she's pushing forward into the chair. She knocks her purse into my knee, sputtering in fury all the time. Good grief. Are the seats assigned beforehand? Are they all already claimed? What a shitty reception on my first social outing here at Manor House. I start for the door, leaning heavily

9

on my cane. Sarah arrives at that moment with her dinner-mates, her three best friends from the building, Hiba, Jeanne, and Mia. Hiba is her very best friend here and Jeanne is probably the person she sees the most because they share a daily scrabble game. Mia is a painter who spends a lot of her time in her bedroom, which she has turned into a studio because the light is so good. Sarah had talked about all three a lot in our correspondence during that long period when I was stuck with my family in my house. "Oh, come sit with us, Lillian," she says, looping an arm around my bicep and leaning in to whisper, "If you don't mind sitting close."

We speak in whispers since the lights are already dimmed. I ask about the unspoken seating rules. "Oh no. Did you try to take someone's seat before I arrived? I bet there was drama." When I tell her what happened, she says, "Sounds like you ran into Elaine. She sits on the aisle, which is actually where her husband Richard used to sit. He died about a year ago and she refuses to sit anywhere but his seat. Like she's saving it for him in case he returns."

"Oh, so it was a sentimental thing. Symbolic. I couldn't understand why she was being so aggressive," I say, rummaging in my bag for the thermos of tea I had packed for myself.

Sarah nods. "It's not uncommon here. Maybe

Elaine feels like it's the last shred of control over her life. First she had to leave the home where she lived all her adult life and move here to Manor House, because she couldn't cope alone with her husband once he started wandering. Then, before they can even adjust to living here, his doctor insists that he be moved into the Assisted Living wing, where there's more support. But within weeks, they say that they can't cope with him there and must put him into what they call – without irony – the Memory Unit."

"You mean the locked dementia wing? You'd think they'd call it the No Memory Unit."

"Exactly. So she gives up her regular life in order to keep them together, but right away they get separated. A few months later he dies. They were together 55 years. And what a good listener he must've been because that woman can talk!" We smile at each other. "When you're around old people more, you'll understand why she's so fierce about keeping a sense of continuity, even if it's just the same ole seat."

I realize that I need to pee even though I went to the bathroom back in Freda's apartment before I came to the screening room. I push past everyone in the row and, damn it, the lights are starting to go down. Luckily there is a restroom right across the hall – I guess the architects knew some older women – and I manage to get back while the opening credits are still running. I'm glad it's an old black and white film so that the credits are upfront, because nowadays in 2009 all the films put them at the end.

I settle into my seat next to Sarah in the half-filled theater, our shoulders touching each other. I lay my sweater over my lap and she snakes her hand under the wool, settling her fingers over my knee. It's only a knee, but I feel a buzz travel up my thigh, creating a warmth between my legs. I tremble. There's something deliciously naughty about our furtive pettings. I slip my own hand under the sweater and rest it lightly over Sarah's. We stay motionless for minutes, concentrating on the delectable sensations, while Marlon Brando passes unseen on the screen.

When the lights go up, our exciting clandestine moments of connection in the dark are over. Sarah introduces me to her two friends. Jeanne apparently slipped out in the middle of the film. Mia, rotund and friendly, shakes my hand. "I'm sorry I can't hang out but I'm waiting for a phone call," she says before jogging out the door of the screening room.

"And this is Hiba," Sarah says. "My bestie in Manor House."

Hiba lays her hands on my shoulders and air-kisses both cheeks. "We have been waiting for your arrival so very long," she says with a musical accent, "I am so glad you're here at last." Her black bob is striped with grey, her embroidered tunic reminds me of a Bedouin tablecloth I used to have, and her smile wins me over immediately.

"You must excuse Mia," Hiba says, "but a friend in Philadelphia is trying to set up an exhibition for Mia at a gallery she works at. So she's been waiting for the friend to call. But I don't have plans this evening. Would you like to join me in my apartment for a drink?" Hiba looks first at Sarah and then at me.

"I'm tempted," I answer, "but I'm afraid that I'm too tired to be much use as a guest. But please invite me again." The truth is that I'm anxious to get to my bathroom for a pee.

Hiba air-kisses me again, Sarah kisses me softly on my forehead, and we go our separate ways.

I return to Freda's apartment alone, exhausted, trying to take it all in. A good hot shower is what I need.

I strip off my clothes and climb into the shower, holding onto the bars that have been installed every which way. Just stepping in over a one-inch lip is a shaky proposition because of my neuropathy. Strange how it acts up when I'm in an emotional state, and these last few days certainly qualify for that. Hanging on to a bar with each hand, I put my foot down cautiously. The last thing I need is to twist my ankle or break my little toe – which is all too easy to do when you can't really feel your foot. But what an improvement on the set-up in my own house. The only shower Bernard and I ever put in was just a pipe with a showerhead screwed on the end, hanging over the tub. It dribbled down unevenly, with one stream squirting right at the shower curtain no matter how we twisted and turned the showerhead. The harrowing part was climbing into the tub. I found myself increasingly doing sponge baths, out of fear of getting in and out.

So this is a special treat. I can stand under this stream until I look pickled. And best of all, unlike in a bath, there are no consequences to my peeing right here under the shower. I run my hand over my body. Okay, sure, it's been years and years since I got it on with anyone else, but I've never neglected my own touch. I'm grateful to the women's movement for that. I can't say I was much of an activist, what with Bernard and the boys, but no one can say I didn't do my share of reading. And there were so many good articles about self-love, about loving our own bodies. If I tell the truth, that was a lifesaver. Life as a widow would've been pretty frustrating without my own fingers.

There's both an overhead and a hand-held shower head in these apartments. The adjustable hand-held is mounted about waist height so that when I sit on the triangular plastic seat that's built into the corner of the shower unit, I can aim it to hit me wherever I want. The switch right next to this corner seat controls the change between the overhead and the hand-held.

I experiment a bit and discover that if I hold on to a bar on either side of the seat, I can slouch down so far that the stream of water hits me right on my pussy. This stream is much more focused than the overhead spray. I aim it above my clitoris, right on the edge of my pelvic bone, and, well, the water does the rest. The spray pounds just right and I get really aroused. And it doesn't take long. Just a minute or two. At a crucial point, I let go of the right bar and rub my clit hard, right where I like it, fantasize about Sarah, and with the water's help, voilà, I have a magnificent orgasm.

Whew. That's the way to end the day. What a relief that there are no children or grandchildren queuing up at the bathroom door, as there were at home.

I lean back, my head against the wall, until my breathing returns to normal. How easy to grab these bars on both sides, to hoist myself up until I'm steady, and then to reach out with one hand to shut off the water. I switch to another bar so that I can carefully step out onto the rug to dry. As my bad foot hits Freda's fluffy bath rug, I can feel the foot tingling. Had I been pushing it against the side of the shower? I can't see my feet from "up here," so it's difficult to judge on my own when I might have done myself damage. As I towel myself dry, I decide I'm okay, if parched. I put on my slippers and go pour myself a tumbler of orange juice, grateful that Sarah has stocked my fridge with the basics.

3. It Takes All Kinds

The next morning I see a man sitting alone at a breakfast table meant for four. Sarah had emailed the night before to say she had stayed up reading and wouldn't be coming down for breakfast. I approach the guy and ask if there is a vacant seat, even though it is plain that there are three available seats. He is a little startled and jumps up from his chair, so that his cloth napkin falls from his lap. He had already extended his hand to me at the same time that he stood up and I had taken it and started to shake it. But even though he is holding on to my hand, he bends down creakily trying to retrieve the napkin, pulling me down with him. This throws me way off balance. I lean heavily on the table, spilling his glass of water which splashes onto the back of his head where he's bending over. At least that makes him let go and I can repossess my hand. Since I've been unconsciously tugging in an attempt to free my hand, once he releases his hold I fall back into a serendipitous chair.

This is more drama than I can handle before I've even had my first cup of tea. "I'm sorry for my part in that shower. No punishment too great for an act of chivalry," I say, trying to smooth over the awkwardness when I see how red his face has gone.

"God loves chivalry," the man says.

Oh damn it. I'm in for it now.

17

"I'm Lillian." Luckily I've fallen into the seat across from him so that there is an empty seat between us on both sides. I like to keep a little space between me and the lord's spokesmen. "I'm staying here for a few weeks."

"I'm Henry Smyth, nice to meet you." He mops the back of his neck with his errant napkin. "I've been living here for six months. Miserable months." He shakes his bald head back and forth, his long thin nose sloping down over thin, colorless lips in a permanent frown.

I wave to the server, whom I've met at a previous meal. "Lewanda, isn't it?"

The young woman, her curves filling out the scrubs she is wearing, smiles briefly. "Yes, that's right." She places a large glass of water in front of me, for which I'm grateful.

I ask for two soft boiled eggs and some toast with my tea. And a nice wedge of lemon on the side. Lewanda nods and leaves. I'm jealous she can walk away. I'd like to abandon the scene as well. But like a good girl I swivel back to face Henry.

In front of him sits a bowl of porridge, a small pitcher of milk, and a cup of coffee. He lifts the milk and pours it into his coffee. "Lord, save me!" he cries out.

Surprised, I wonder if I should flee. What a strange fucking reaction.

"Sorry," he says. "Dumb move. I drink my

coffee black. Meant the milk for my porridge. Was flustered. You know. The napkin. The water. You. The devil took over the pitcher."

"I apologize again," I say.

He waves at Lewanda, pointing at his coffee. She brings over the pot, but he points, stabbing his finger towards his now cream-colored drink and muttering. Who could possibly understand the problem from his inarticulate gestures? She doesn't. In fact, she steps back one step. I don't blame her, considering how his frustration is pouring out like livid lava.

I intervene, although the last thing I want is to be a social worker or translator so early in the morning. "He wants a clean coffee cup so he can have black coffee."

Lewanda returns with a clean cup and my breakfast. I pick up a spoon to have a go at the soft-boiled eggs when this Henry Smyth leans way over in my direction, pointing his finger upwards, and shaking it back and forth – no, no, no – as he tsks at me. "You wouldn't eat without saying grace to our Lord Jesus Christ, now would you?"

I look around. My appetite has evaporated. All I want is some distance between me and the Christian. Perhaps staying here at Manor House is a bad idea. Perhaps I've lived alone much too long to have patience for this crap.

"You wouldn't skip grace, would you? Not a

nice lady like you."

I look the man right in the face. "Oh yes, I would. I don't have anything to do with all of that at all."

I squeeze my lemon into my tea and butter my toast. If I ate the eggs now I'd vomit. I gobble the bread as fast as I can. But, damn if he isn't mumbling something liturgical at me from across the table. I keep my eyes down until I hear sniffling. When I quickly glance up, it's clear that he's crying.

If ever I needed a prayer, I think, it would be now. Lord, do an abracadabra and get me the hell out of here. I twist to see if I can locate Sarah, but no luck. Of course not! I forgot for a second that she said she wouldn't be coming down.

"No one ever sits with me. Or talks with me. Even though I'm doing the Lord's good work. They all hate me. They won't..." and he stops to use the multi-purpose napkin to blow his dripping nose. I wonder how reliable the laundry service is at Manor House. "I was only here a few weeks. They decided. All of them." He stands up, his coffee untouched. "God bless you and keep you in His Holy embrace. You'll excuse me." And he hurries away.

I watch him until he's out of sight, then I struggle up, leaning heavily on my cane, and hurry to my apartment as exhausted as if it were the end, not the start, of the day. I'm rushing not only for the shelter of my rooms, but also for the use of the bathroom. Yet again. I've always been what Freda calls a "pisher," one who takes frequent leaks. But my frequency seems to have hit an upturn this week. When I finish with the bathroom, I call Freda in Florida, as I had promised I would do. She tells me how she and Lenny are doing at their cousin's house.

"You vouldn't believe how our Lenny is loving the Florida, in his own vay. He vants to go to a town they are calling Sarasota. It has itself the only Amish beach resort anyvere. But it's not the beach for our Lenny. No, he has heard they have in the South Florida Museum the world's best collection of dreck fossils. You know "dreck"? It's poop. Number two. He thinks the whole state is like a comic dream. But enough with that, how's by you?"

"Let me keep up the Jewish tradition and answer your question with a question. So who is this Christian guy, Henry Smyth?"

"*Oy gevalt*. A sad guy, *meshugenah*, I'm sorry to say. Have you met him?"

"I sat with him at breakfast. He sits alone. The others have a boycott on him, he says. Is it true? That would be a mean thing to do, even if he could win the Gold Medal for Most Annoying."

"It is mean, you are right, but he brings this upon himself. He hates everyvon. The vomen he hates. The workers, he hates. The non-Christians, he hates. The Christians who aren't fundamentalists, he hates. And man oh man does he hate the Black people. May you never be on the wrong side of this *schlepper*," she says prophetically. "He makes trouble for all the nice ones."

4. The Bladder Speaks

Now that I've been in Manor House for five days, I can finally breathe, at least until the next time I get the urinary urge. I wish I could figure out how to bring this problem up when I'm talking to Sarah. It shouldn't be a secret – I mean we're old enough to be sharing physical problems.

Other than the constant sprints to the bathroom, I'm loving it here. On the one hand, since Freda's apartment is not my home and her stuff is not my stuff, I feel like a guest, a transient. But on the other hand, since it isn't my home and my stuff, I feel 1,000 pounds lighter, like I've thrown off unwanted baggage and gone on vacation. No depressed, lethargic son. No ditzy daughter-in-law. No freaked out grandkids. No necessity to look around my place at my myriad *tchotchkes* with the thought that to anyone else, they are just junk knick-knacks. The little statue of the peeing boy – Bernard bought that in Belgium during the War. The *papier-mâché* butterflies – we purchased them from a street artist in LA. I've helped clear out enough homes of people who have died to know that these things lose all their meaning once they're no longer with their owner. It's a relief not to have to dust them. Or to have to concern myself about the mildew in the basement or the weeds breaking up the front steps. My house forces me into a constant state of guilt: it wants more attention from me than I'm able to bestow. Just like my son and his family.

Freda's apartment is an escape pod. I don't have to inhale the fumes of Lee's diapers or Lisa's teeny-bopper perfume. I don't have to watch Leon squeezing his pimples or put up with his video game explosions at the dining table. Best of all, I'm not assailed with the creaking of Michael and Emily's bed through the wall of my bedroom.

Even the good burdens, like Bernard and our dead son Norman, are in exile. The photos here are not my photos. The table isn't our table. There are no heavy memories around me. I'm getting comfy and I'm digging being able to close the door once again. I haven't felt this relaxed in a place since "the invasion," as Sarah called it, when my son, daughter-in-law, and three grandkids turned up on my doorstep broke, insisting on moving in. It might not have been such a catastrophe if it hadn't come quite literally on the day I'd decided to unload the house so I could afford to move into Manor House. Not the least because I'm on the edge of a new romance with a wonderful woman, unexpected at this time in my life. A woman!

Anyway, the environment in Manor House is amazing. Every aspect of the set-up here takes the needs of seniors into account. All the handrails and other safety stuff give me a sense of security. I spend a lot of time walking around Freda's apartment, opening kitchen cupboards, getting to know where everything is. Then I fall asleep with a sense of freedom, probably similar to that of a teenager who has moved into her first apartment.

Next morning, feeling self-indulgent after getting up for an early morning pee, I decide to go back to sleep. Why let my bladder define my morning? The bed is firm and I doze off within minutes. My foot is painful, but I'm used to that. Unfortunately heaven doesn't last long: The ringer of Freda's phone, set on a senior-super-loud level because Freda is hard of hearing, is a rough awakening. Oh damn it. I've got to figure out how to change the settings. I peel my head up from the exuberantly ruffled pillow cases Freda likes to embroider and throw my arm in the general direction of the noise, grabbing the receiver on my first try.

"Hello?"

"Mum, listen, we need you today." Michael's voice is like a glass shard in the ear. It isn't only the ringer that is set for the hard of hearing. The speaker level is an assault, too. "I've got an informational meeting with a guy at a different startup and Emily has to take Lee to the doctor's. Can you come over and babysit when the kids get home from school?"

"I'm fine, Michael. Thanks for asking." My voice is creaky with sleep. I reach over for the glass of water I keep next to the bed and take a huge sip.

"Oh right, sorry. How are ya, Mum?"

"Enjoying myself immensely, Michael. And no, I can't babysit. Or rather I won't. Think of me as abroad for six weeks. Isn't that what I told you?"

"But you're not abroad, damn it." I have to hold the handset away from my head so that my son's irritation doesn't bust my eardrum.

"In any event, I have plans this afternoon."

"Can't you change them?" Now he's almost yelling.

I raise my voice in return. "I imagine I could change them, but I don't intend to, Michael. You should have developed a Plan B as soon as I told you that I'd be away for six weeks."

"Well, I've got other things on my mind." Now he's screaming, the noise cascading out of the receiver that I'm holding at arm's length, "As you must know only too well."

"Yes, I know the feeling!" My own volume is also out of control.

"Some grandmother you're turning out to be."

Luckily my mouth does not speak my thoughts: *Some shitty son you turned out to be. Quit squatting in my house so that I can sell it and live the life I want in my final years.* While trying to come up with a more polite but honest retort, I'm distracted by a light knocking on my door. That gives me an excuse. "I've got to run, Michael, someone's here.

Good luck with that informational session, or whatever it's called. Give my love."

I grab my robe and my cane and approach the peephole. It's Emmanuel.

"Emmanuel?"

"I was passing by your door and heard raised voices. I am making sure everything's okay."

"I'm fine, Emmanuel. Oh my goodness? Is it time for breakfast?"

"Yes, they stop serving at 9:30."

"Damn. Somehow that slipped by me. I'll get dressed right away and get down there. Thanks."

"Designated mealtimes," I say to Sarah as we settle into a corner table with our eggs and biscuits and my tall glass of juice, "are about the worst aspect of living here. I loved eating whenever I wanted, whatever I wanted." The table posse culture didn't apply to breakfast, so it was no problem for Sarah and me to eat breakfast together.

"I know what you mean," Sarah says. "Working at the library all those years, I never knew what shift I'd be on. That drove Alexandra crazy. She liked eating three meals a day, and I usually just had a meal before work, whenever that might be, and another after. She wanted us to eat together, but that didn't really work for me."

Sarah is quiet for a minute. I watch her face; watch the lines in her leathery skin change their pattern as a series of emotions pass over it.

"Tell me more about how things ended with Alexandra. All I know is that she left you for a young horse trainer – wasn't she named Delores? – just three weeks after her first riding lesson."

"Yeah, that's the short version. Actually, it happened the very night that we had celebrated our 25th anniversary with a gaggle of long-time friends. Alexandra's suitcases had actually been packed and secretly put in the trunk of her car, making the trip with us to the restaurant.

"'I didn't want to spoil everyone's evening,' she told me when we pulled up to the front of the house, 'but this is it. I'm finished. I'm moving to the farm with Delores.' She had leaned over for a good-bye kiss, the kind of habitual smooch long-time couples exchange on departure. I'm not ashamed to say that I slapped her across the face. 'Screw you,' I said. 'Nice anniversary gift.'"

A whiff of pain blows through Sarah's expression as she recites what happened. "The night that Alexandra dumped me was the night I started thinking about senior housing. It was one of those lessons we all get periodically that life is short, that everything can change on a dime. What I call a slap in the face with a dead fish. It's always upsetting to remember that our greatest supports are too wobbly to totally depend on. I thought I'd be able to count on Alexandra forever. So that's when I started researching where I could live independently, but at the same time begin building a cool circle of friends."

"And have you found the right people here?"

"I was one of the youngest people here when I moved in. And I gravitated right to Freda and Lenny – I had met them years ago in some political group. And then I met Hiba. She was pretty isolated because she's an immigrant from Ramallah, left her family behind when she married an American, and then was widowed a couple of years ago."

"Ramallah?"

"It's in Palestine. The West Bank."

"Of course!"

"And then Hiba got friends with Mia – Hiba loves Mia's artwork – and I connected with her too. Mia's work is abstract, but it's all about deserts. She spent a few years in Arizona, in the Chihuahuan Desert, and made several visits to Egypt's Sinai Desert, where Hiba has also been. A few months later I met Jeanne separately, in the games room, where she challenged me to a round of scrabble. Months later she told me that someone had mentioned that I was a retired librarian and she crossed her fingers, hoping I would be a worthy opponent. The daily game with her is really important to me. Basically it's the only regular commitment I have. She's the only one I know absolutely that I'll be seeing every day – at least until dinner time. Hiba's my best friend, but Jeanne is my anchor. I introduced her to the others and they liked her too. That's how we became a dinner foursome. Anyway, I do feel like my grand plan is coming together. Except that…"

Sarah interrupts herself, laughing quietly. "What is it?" I ask.

Sarah waits a full five seconds, as if she's getting up her nerve. She reaches over and runs one finger from my shoulder to my wrist. I shiver. A simple thing like that totally changes the mood – and it's so hot – downright sizzling. "It's been five or six days, now, since you came to stay here. So near, but still so far away."

And now I'm embarrassed. I look down at my plate, but then Sarah closes her hand over mine. "I don't mean to put you on the spot…"

It's time for me to admit what I've been hiding. "It's not that. It's just that I've had a bit of a problem since I got here which is, well, which is holding me back. In the romance department, I mean."

Sarah continues to hold my hand, puzzled, cocking her head as she waits for the explanation.

I explain. "It's stupid, I know. About a week ago I developed the most awful case of dry mouth. So to deal with the dry mouth I'm drinking constantly which makes me run to the bathroom all day and all night, as you've probably noticed. It doesn't make me feel very sexy. Believe me, in between gulping liquids and running to the loo, I can't think of anything but you. Seriously, I've been in a state of anticipation ever since I decided to come here for six weeks – I mean anticipation about us."

"Do you know what's causing it? The dry mouth, I mean, not the anticipation."

"The problem is my doctor's back in my old neighborhood and my son's family all use her too. They're always at the clinic with one kid or other. I'm not ready to run into them at this point, trust me."

"I had a friend went through that whole dry mouth thing when his doctor changed his prescription."

"What? Wait a minute; that could explain it. I just started taking a blood pressure pill. Like a couple of days before I moved here. Could it be that? Just that? Something so easy to fix?"

I jump up. "Got to call my doctor."

"Wait! Call your pharmacist. They know side effects better."

5. Talkative Dinner-Mate

Two days later, after a Manor House lunchtime poetry reading, I took a deep breath before asking Sarah, "How about coming to my place after dinner tonight for dessert?" I tried to put on my most coquettish face, as I added, "Well, let's say dessert plus, well, breakfast."

"At last! What a tempting offer. Yes, yes, yes."

After confirming with the pharmacist that the new blood pressure medicine I was taking often caused, he said, "excessive dehydration and urination," and after contacting my doctor's office to ask for an alternative, I had taken the Manor House shuttle to the local pharmacy to pick up the new prescription.

"I need something to stop the constant peeing right now," I told the pharmacist, "just something over-the-counter if you've got it. Just to use for tonight, tomorrow, till my body adjusts to the other stuff."

"You'll feel the difference with the new pill in a few days, but meanwhile, you can try this medication." He handed me a box. "It stops that urgent feeling. But, listen, there may be a problem with the script. Medicare may give you aggro about ordering two different blood pressure meds in the same month. There's no real way to know in advance."

"I'll fight that when the time comes," I said. "In the meantime, I look forward to escaping the four walls of my toilet prison."

"Yep," he giggled, "sounds like urine trouble."

It is only on my way back to Manor House that I get the pun. I wonder how many times he's made the same crack.

Meanwhile, the afternoon before the evening, I sauté some "herbs" in a full stick of butter, which, after straining out the now-limp herbs, I use to bake some thick brownies. I set them out to cool. I go to the folding chair in the bedroom that I've been using to pile my stuff on since most other surfaces are crowded with Freda's belongings. I find the boxed present for Sarah, and miraculously it hasn't lost the coating of my granddaughter's glitter.

I go down to dinner early, hoping to find a random seat so that I won't have to sit at Henry Smyth's table. Coincidentally, there is a seat next to Elaine and for a moment I wonder if she's saving this seat out of respect for her departed spouse.

"May I sit here?"

Elaine looks up with a tentative smile. She doesn't seem to recognize me from that incident in the movie room. "I don't see why not. Usually Gladys sits there, but she's away in Mexico visiting her son and his wife and the grandkids." Man does she talk fast. Like a machine gun. "I'll tell you this. I wouldn't want to be in a foreign country with those grandchildren. They're twins, boys, and one is worse than the next. Richard – that's my husband, my late husband – Richard always felt there was something funny about twins. Can you imagine how upset Gladys was when I told her that? She said it was news to her and she wasn't taking advice from Richard about her own relatives. And I said, Of course you're not taking advice from Richard. He passed away, remember? Wait a minute, have you met Gladys?"

I'm still standing, leaning forward uncomfortably so that I can hear her tirade over the dining room noise. "No, and I haven't formally met you either. My name is Lillian. Nice to meet you."

"I feel I've met you before," Elaine says, "but I can't remember where. Please sit down." I hang my sweater on the back of the chair and then prop my cane on top. As I lower into my seat she asks me, "Are you a new resident?"

"No, I'm a guest for six weeks. I'm staying in Freda's apartment while she and her brother are in Florida. I want to move in but I have some family business to sort out before I can do that."

"I see. Not sure why you'd want to move into a place like this. I mean with the Assisted Living Unit next door. The Memory Unit across the courtyard. The whole bleak future is hovering. You didn't know my Richard, did you? Well, they had him ricocheting from one facility to the other and in the end he just got worse and I said to him, not that he was able to listen or concentrate by then, that we probably would have been better off staying home, although my social worker wouldn't hear of it and claimed she was looking out for me. So what, I said to her, so what if Richard gets confused now and again. So what if he slips out of the house in his PJs at all hours. I can take care of him like I always have. That's how I am. But oh no, she said we'd be better off here and so we came and he is gone."

Awkward. Weird to know part of this history, while she doesn't know I know. I say, "It's different for everyone, don't you think? At least the people who buy a place here have enough money to make that choice. As for me, I can't wait to sell my house and move here. I'm very sick of having so many steps up to my front door, of dealing with the leak in the roof, with the mildew in the basement, with hiring people to tend the yard. The idea of a small, updated little flat, well that appeals to me."

"I'm in a two-bedroom," Elaine said.

"That must feel more spacious."

"No, at this point, it feels lonely. I only got a two-bedroom because I was married when I came here and that's how you're able to request one. Of course it's much more expensive, but when it came to Richard, I just wasn't going to scrimp. That's the way I am. I could have bought shoulder lamb chops like everyone else did, but no, only the best for my

Richard. I bought ribs, even though they were so expensive, it meant I had to use rags instead of pads, you'll excuse my language. He complained. Said he liked the shoulder cut better, grew up with them, but I knew the man. He was trying to be nice to me. Even after dinner he'd say he was still hungry, the ribs were too small. Oh my Richard. He was modest. But even though I got us a two-bedroom, and they're pretty rare in Manor House, I believe I mentioned to you earlier that my husband died this year. In the Memory Unit."

Whew. This woman can race from sentence to sentence in the time it takes another person to burp. "My condolences. I'm so sorry to hear that."

"He had really lost it. No question about it. And he lost it before we ever got here, but I was pretty good at covering for him. I knew he was going downhill a couple of years ago, when he was about 88. That's when I realized we were doomed. 'Cause he stopped smoking."

"Sounds like he hadn't lost his willpower, at least."

"No, it wasn't that. He'd been smoking all his life. Even back when we were courting in high school. But one day he wakes up and completely forgets that he smokes.

"So what's with all these ashtrays? he asks me. And lighters everywhere. Are we having guests?

"You smoke, I tell him. No I don't, he says. I

never smoked. I don't smoke. So I just left it at that. They say it's no use arguing with them. Gave all the ashtrays to a neighbor after a few weeks passed and he didn't go back to the cigarettes. You might think it was a good thing, but that's the point at which I said, Okay, time for us to move out of our house. We're in trouble."

Lewanda arrives to take our order, while I give the menu the once-over. Manor House offers two different entrees each night – one meat and one either fish or veggie. They also have two regulars that are always available: two hotdogs with beans, or mac and cheese with a side of cole slaw.

There were folks, Sarah had told me, who had the same thing night after night after night. I can totally understand that, not being much of a gourmet myself. All those years of living alone, I got used to cooking something, a meatloaf say, and eating it all week. If it was one of my favorites, then it didn't bother me and there was no one else around to object.

I order the steak tips and mashed potatoes and begin to work on the little side salad each diner is served. Two friends of Elaine's, Frannie and Mimi, arrive and wave their hands towards Lewanda, ready to order. Although Elaine introduces me, they mainly talk among themselves. Or rather, Elaine talks at them. Relentlessly, incessantly. That's fine with me. I've got the evening to think about, to fantasize about, to plan in my head. This is going to be a big night for Sarah and me.

6. Puff the Magic Brownie

At 7:00, Sarah knocks twice on my door. Finally I've got an occasion to dress for, and I open the door, wrapped in the long satin bathrobe in silver I bought online the day I accepted Freda's invitation to stay here. What a boon Internet shopping is for "gimps and crips," as one friend with bad scoliosis likes to say. A polished silver headband secures my long white hair, loose down my back for the occasion.

I open the door to find Sarah holding out a bouquet of daffodils, but she is so astonished by this new, unexpected image of me that she neglects to hand them over. I had been hoping she'd have this kind of reaction – and not think that I'm being a foolish old woman trying to tart up. Plus, I was nervous: who knows what women wear in bed with each other. I don't.

I take the flowers from Sarah's hand – "For me?" – and only then, to my self-centered embarrassment, do I notice how Sarah is dressed. Starched, ruffled, bright white tuxedo shirt with black cufflinks tucked into handsome black slacks over patent leather boots.

"Well, well," I say in my most seductive voice. "Someone cleans up nicely. What a fine-looking twosome we make – you're ready for the opera and I'm heading for the boudoir. Come in before someone sees us."

"So what if they do?"

"As they say in Yiddish: Love is blind; jealousy sees too much. I don't want the neighbors' envy on my conscience."

Sarah only takes a couple of steps inside before she stops – a mixture of a smile and surprise taking hold. The apartment is glowing. I've changed some table lamp bulbs to red bulbs, and then Emmanuel helped me string a length of pink fairy lights over the bed. He was almost giggling the whole time, but he didn't pry. I'm sure the people who work in Manor House could fill the Grand Canyon with the secrets they know about residents.

"I'm not going to offer you wine or any drink other than tea," I say. "Do you know why?" Of course she doesn't.

"Because I baked pot brownies and I'm hoping you'll agree to split one with me."

"Are you a doper?" Sarah asks.

"The truth? I am, big-time."

Sarah laughs, shaking her head. "Well, I'll be. Me too! Have been since the 60s." She reaches into her bag and pulls out a leather pouch, waving it around. It must be her stash. "Great minds," she says.

"Me, it's just since Bernard died. I was in an eight-week bereavement group – we called ourselves the Grief Girls. We've kept meeting monthly all these years after the official group ended. Well, some of us have, anyways. One of the young women, her name's Judy, smokes more or less all day, every day. Believe me, we shared painful, intimate things in the group, so when she brought a couple of joints one evening, she convinced us to share those too. And the rest is history. I found it really eases the discomfort of my neuropathy; I mean it's a fuckin' miracle drug. And you know what? The Grief Girls are meeting in a few weeks. So if these brownies are potent – hope you don't mind being a guinea pig because it's the first time I've made them – then I'll take some to try with the girls."

While I'm talking, Sarah sits down on the couch. She's got an indulgent smile, so I ask, "What's up?"

"My god, woman. I've never heard you talk so fast for so long since I met you. So, if you ask me, I think the brownie's a great idea. Maybe it'll make you so mellow that I'll get you to come over here and sit next to me." She pats the couch.

I laugh. "Not yet. I've got tea to make and music to choose. Better yet, why don't you choose a CD." I nod towards the little pile I brought with me from home. Don't get me wrong, I love Freda and Lenny to death, but their own stand of CDs ranges from Streisand to Yiddish musicals. I leave her to it while I go make a pot of sweet mint tea, Moroccan-style. I don't have Sarah's favorites: she's mentioned Ella Fitzgerald and Alberta Hunter – but I have mine. On top is Debussy, followed by the Ink Spots, the Andrews Sisters, The Platters, Frank Sinatra, and Harry James. She doesn't hesitate for a second: The Ink Spots.

I bring out the little wheeled tray-table I brought from home for moving things from room to room without losing my balance. On it I've placed Freda's familiar teapot and cups, along with one brownie split in half on a little dessert plate. In the center is a vase with the daffodils, especially beautiful bathed in the reddish light. "Let's dig in before we drink the tea," I suggest, "because these can take about an hour or more before they hit."

"Well aren't you the wolf in sheep's clothing," says Sarah. "'Before they hit!' You really are a doper, complete with the lingo. I love a woman who's full of surprises."

We raise up our brownies as I make a toast, "To a special evening!" We gobble them down as quickly as possible to minimize the taste of the plant leavings that I didn't manage to strain out of the butter I sautéed the weed in.

Finally, I put my cane against the arm of the couch and sit down near her. We sip our tea and listen to the Ink Spots quietly singing *Whispering Grass*. "I've got something for you," I say, opening the drawer in the coffee table in front of us, where I had put her gift earlier. "I've had this present for you since I came, but this is the first really relaxed private time we've had together."

She rests the gift bag on her lap. "Let me ask something first. Am I to understand that you're feeling better now? That, uh, that problem is not getting in your way anymore?"

"Yes, and it's thanks to you. Notice that I'm not running to pee and I'm only drinking like anyone else. So glad that you suggested I call my pharmacist. Smart move. He dealt with it immediately. So, with that obstacle out of the way, please open your gift."

Sarah smiles as she reaches in the bag and draws out the glittery box. She looks up, quizzical. "My granddaughter's art supplies finally came in handy," I say. Sarah puts it down on the coffee table and slowly slips off the ribbon and unwraps the little cardboard box. Inside is a smaller blue velvet box, the kind that jewelry comes in and for a moment she is perplexed. I giggle.

She flips open the top and is still puzzled. Inside are two penny-sized circles of jade set in rings of filigreed silver, and attached to elasticized woven ribbons.

"Cufflinks of some sort?"

"Nope."

She picks one up and suddenly she gets it. "Are these for my pigtails?"

"Yes!"

"Like glorified rubber bands – only gorgeous?"

"Yes! I had them made for you."

"And you noticed that the only jewelry I wear is jade and silver?"

"Yes!"

Finally I've managed to blow Sarah's mind. She's stunned.

"Do you like them, Sarah? A Native American craftswoman works at a shop near my house. I described what I wanted and it turned out she had made some, but with plastic beads. She's got friends who wear decorated braids."

"Come here," Sarah says, putting her arms around me. I look right into her eyes and find myself flushing. She kisses my forehead, down my nose, and lightly on my lips. The Ink Spots start singing *I'm Beginning to See the Light*. I struggle up, and reach out my hand. "Do you dance? I don't even know if you dance."

Sarah springs up, almost spilling the braid decorators on the floor. She lays them carefully in the center of the coffee table. "Do I *dance*? Do *I* dance?" She repeats herself with a different emphasis. "How'd you like to learn the Lesbian Two-Step?"

For a nano-second I pause. This is the first time Sarah has said the word "lesbian" in reference to us. It jars, but not in a bad way. It just reminds me how different our lives have been. I've never been involved with a woman before, but Sarah has identified as a lesbian all her life. The word is as common to her as "widow" is to me. I shake myself out of these thoughts as Sarah comes around the table and takes my hand.

Her eyes caress my eyes as she wraps her right arm around my back. Bernard and I used to dance quite a bit. It's so great to feel that Sarah knows just what she's doing. For a moment we don't move, but we are both beaming.

She starts shifting her weight from foot to foot and I match her. We're swaying, not moving, until with an expert switch, Sarah puts her own weight on her left leg and moves mine onto my right. Sarah taps her foot each time she switches to the other foot. I'm a good follower and her lead is easy to read. Sarah subtly increases the motion until we are actually dancing. Of course there's not much room in Freda's living room, so our steps are tiny. Really we're practically dancing in place – but we sure are dancing. Sway, tap, sway, tap: it works perfectly. *We* work perfectly.

The song ends but we don't move. One of my favorite cuts comes on: *I'll Get By – As Long as I Have You*. Sarah pulls me closer. Her right thigh is between my legs and I shiver as my most sensitive spot rests on the muscle in Sarah's leg. So *that's* why it's called the Lesbian Two-Step! I wrap my left hand delicately around the back of Sarah's neck. She trembles. This is unbelievable. I've made this confident, experienced woman I desire tremble! She presses her breasts against mine even more firmly as we continue dancing. I realize that my limp has faded. I'm not thinking of any of my deficits. Not my neuropathy, not my sagging butt, my floppy upper arms, or my sloping 84-year-old back. I'm just surrendering to Sarah's lead and getting lost in the dance.

The Ink Spots start singing *Java Jive*. This has got to be the most upbeat of all their hits. It's not the right beat for the grindy Lesbian Two-Step. "Oh how Bernard and I used to jitterbug to this," I say, breaking the quiet moment.

"So did Alexandra and I."

As we stand there holding each other, I realize that my leg is too tired to go on. "Tea?"

"Sure, but only if you sit right next to me."

Like kids we sit side by side, pressing against each other where we are touching, from shoulder to hip, as if we're trying to meld together. Suddenly I realize that I'm super-high.

"Hey, I think the brownie has hit!" I pick up my now tepid tea and gulp it down.

She stops moving altogether for a second, lifting her gaze to the ceiling in concentration, and then says, "Me too! Thirsty, too." She drinks up her tea as well.

We relax back in the sofa. I snuggle into her arm and look up at her. For a moment the room spins. "I'm a bit dizzy," I murmur. "High and dizzy."

She holds me closer and I feel fine again. It's a bit awkward, because it's time for one of us to make a move. We both sigh. Slowly I realize that Sarah is not going to be that someone.

"You're waiting for me, aren't you?"

She nods. "I am."

"It's because I'm straight?"

"Are you straight, Lillian?"

"Well, you know. Inexperienced with women, let's say. Feminine. Never attracted to a woman before."

"Yes, that's part of it. But it's also because I'm a butch, and I've learned to be paranoid."

"Maybe I'm higher than I thought, but what's the connection between butch and paranoia?"

"When I was young, really young, I had two different bad experiences with straight women."

"Because they didn't know what they were doing?"

"Oh no, not that. Because afterwards they claimed to regret sleeping with me. I guess they blamed me when they ran into the brick wall of prejudice and ostracism. One even said I seduced her. In a bad sense. That's what she told her parents when they threatened to disown her."

"How awful!"

"It was how things were. I've heard plenty of stories from friends. When I was just starting out at my first library job, I met an older dyke who had been fired from a different branch because some disgruntled employee of hers made nasty accusations about her behavior in the bathroom. It was a lie, but the fear never left me. For many years I didn't go into the ladies' room at the library unless it was completely empty. I'd loiter in the hall till no one was in there and rush in and out."

"But surely you don't think that I'd… I mean, we're grown-ups now. And it's another era."

"Lillian, this isn't about you. This is about my long-lived life. This is about leftover scars from before the gay movement. You don't know about living in the closet, about being called mentally ill in the official therapy books, about all the violence I faced as a young dyke. This is about my history, not your present."

"I know about homophobia and about the Christian fundamentalists, but that's recent history. Since I met you I've tried to read everything about gay people in the newspapers. But of course I don't really know much about lesbian life in the 40s and 50s."

"Have you ever experienced forbidden love, Lillian? Of any kind?" The tone of her voice has changed, like she's speaking to someone slow-witted.

"I'm afraid my sexual timeline is pretty thin. I dated a couple of guys before Bernard and a couple of guys after Barnard, but those affairs weren't fraught and they weren't even passionate."

I pause, trying to figure out how to recapture our sexy mood and how to move things forward. I decide to just speak the truth. "All I know is that I long for you, a longing that I recognize. I felt it when I met Bernard, but that was the only time. He died so many years ago. I never thought I'd feel this again in my life. But I have no doubts, Sarah. This is where I want to be."

I bury my face in her neck. "Please hold me. And let me hold you." Sarah is still stiff, looking abstractly across the room over my head. I cup the side of her cheek softly and move her face to me. When I can, I touch her lips with mine, delicately, and hold still.

When that does not change the mood, I shift my position. Facing her, I use my tongue to moisten first my lips and then hers. With my hand behind her head, I pull her down and kiss her with a passion that surprises me. She feels it, though, because she leans in and squeezes me and kisses me back.

We barely stop for air before suddenly my leg cramps up. "Shit! My leg can't take this position anymore."

"And I'm terribly thirsty." Sarah reaches for her cup of tea, now cold, but almost misses the handle. "And pretty damned stoned."

"At last I've come into my own in the kitchen. Never could bake very well, but finally I've found my hidden talent. They call them edibles."

Sarah leans down and bites playfully at my earlobe. "You're a bit of an edible yourself."

7. 84 in Satin

"Would you like to stay overnight?"

"Yes, I would. But no pressure. It would be brilliant to stretch out on a bed together, especially with you in that sexy satin robe. Why don't you use your bathroom first and then I will."

For the third time since she arrived I take a leak. But this time I brush my teeth and notice how smeared my makeup is. I rarely bother anymore, but I thought I'd make a special effort tonight. I remove what is left of the eye shadow and mascara.

"It's all yours now." I'm limping heavily now I realize. My legs are no longer accustomed to dancing – I must build them up. "Your towels are the blue ones. Meanwhile I'll put things away in the kitchen. Do you want a glass of water in the bedroom?"

"Yes please. I need to take my pills anyway." Sarah picks up her backpack and heads for the bathroom. She is in there so long that I finish the dishes, straighten the living room, and take glasses of water into the bedroom. I shed my robe, lay it over a chair, and hope she likes the matching long-sleeve satin nightgown of the same champagne color that I have had under it. I sit up against the headboard, with the covers folded down.

What will it be like to spend the night next to another body? I haven't cuddled all night with anyone for many years – except one night with my granddaughter Lisa when she was afraid of a storm – and that doesn't count. I hope my body doesn't embarrass me – doesn't twitch or cramp or fart. I hope Sarah likes to spoon.

"Can I come out?" Sarah calls as she opens the bathroom door to a nearly dark living room.

"Yes, I'm in bed already."

I gasp when I see Sarah with her pre-Raphaelite cascade of waves. She has unraveled her braids and has brushed her hair so that it is wild and free.

"Of course! I never thought about the fact that you have long hair inside those pigtails. Of course you must brush it out every night. How very beautiful you are. Dante Gabriel Rossetti is probably eating his heart out right now."

Sarah is embarrassed. "Beautiful has never been my goal," she mumbles. I'm sure people have told her how handsome she is, but apparently 'beautiful' isn't a term she hears often. "Anyway, the worms have long ago taken care of Dante Gabriel Rossetti's heart."

"And flannel pajamas! I forgot all about them, but next time I'm shopping I'm going to get some too. They look so comfy."

"I've worn them all my life. My dad and I used to have matching pairs." She is still standing at the doorway.

"Are you joining me?" I lift the corner of the

blankets on the side next to me.

Sarah walks cautiously towards the bed. "I'm still pretty wrecked from that brownie, aren't you?"

"Are you kidding? I got lost about three times going from the living room to the kitchen. I almost decided to leave everything where it was, especially when I remembered what Freda said to me once when I said she couldn't visit my house because it was such a mess after the kids moved in. She said, "Housework probably can't kill you, but vy take a chance.""

Laughing, Sarah makes her way gingerly to the bed and climbs in. I tell her, "Forgive me. I know it's not very sexy, but I've got to lay flat to do my neuropathy stretches. If I don't, I'll be paralytic tomorrow. You might as well know the truth. After all, a young person of 79 like you…"

Sarah smiles. "Just do what you want to do," – she turns on her stomach, her face towards me – "and I'll lie here and learn."

I stretch out my legs under the covers, pointing my toes and then flexing my feet. I concentrate on doing flutter kicks and then short leg lifts. When I finally exhale, I turn to meet Sarah's eyes.

I take a big breath. I've been practicing what I want to say. "I feel like we need to have two conversations," I begin.

Sarah giggles. "Wow, you're a natural at this lesbian thing! That's what we do: first we move in together and then we talk, talk, analyze, and review."

There it was again. The L word.

"I figure we're each making a lot of assumptions about what's going on between us and it might be worth comparing notes."

"I agree," says Sarah. "So that's the first topic. What's the second?"

"Seems like we really ought to have an organ recital before we start bouncing around this bed."

"Organ recital?"

"Yeah, that's what Freda and I do nearly every morning. Like maybe, say, 'Here's what the podiatrist said about my foot cramps. Or, I can't lie on my right side because my hip's acting up. How's your bladder infection?' You know, organ recital."

Sarah cracks up. "Great term! Absolutely right. I want to hear about every ache and pain before we start making magic. Which conversation do you want to have first?"

"I think the relationship one comes before the head-to-toe inspection, no? Damn it, if we were in our 20s, we'd be bouncing on the bed before we knew each other's names, but somehow at 84 it feels like the stakes are a smidge higher."

Having decided to talk, we both fall silent, laying there facing each other. Smiling, I stroke Sarah's cheek lightly until she takes my hand and presses the palm to her lips. She nibbles at the skin in the center of my hand, exposing an erogenous zone I never knew I had. Sarah doesn't stop with the palm; she works her lips past the fleshy part to kiss the inside of my wrist. "Oh!" she says and pulls away. "Are you wearing perfume?"

"Now I'm embarrassed at getting all beautified for you!"

"It's not that, Lillian. It smells wonderful but it doesn't taste so great."

"You're kissing me places I didn't expect to be kissed."

"Expect no inch to go unkissed."

I have no idea how to react to such a radical statement. The idea of another person knowing and loving every inch of me blows my mind. Bernard always kept to the main regions.

Sarah slips the arm she is lying on under my head, raising me off the pillow. She rolls over and kisses me on my lips. The kiss drives out all thoughts of Bernard, who scarcely could be said to have explored every nook and cranny of my body. Sarah's kiss stokes my appetite. But Sarah doesn't linger at my mouth for long. She hoists herself onto her elbow and kisses her way to my ear where she licks around the lobe before drawing her tongue across the back of my ear.

I find myself fighting for breath as my body tingles in a way I barely remember. Remember? Who am I kidding? No one in my life has ever licked the back of my ear. Ever. Or dug their teeth into my scalp delicately the way Sarah is doing now, as she cups her hands around my skull, controlling my head and my excitement. Waves of arousal take over my emotions. Without warning, I burst into tears.

Sarah stops what she is doing and holds me close to her breasts until I stop crying. Somewhere in the middle of my sniffles I do manage to choke out, "Happy crying. Not sad crying." Sarah laughs. "Yes, I know."

8. Fundamentalist Threats

For the third time, I sit down to eat at the table with Elaine and Elaine's two friends. Mimi favors glittery sweat suits à la Florida circa 1985, and Frannie, older than the other two, is either growing out her grey hair or has forgotten her roots of two or three inches. The rest is a faded strawberry red. It was either this table or the table of the Christian, who continues to sit alone meal after meal. "Why doesn't Henry ever have any table mates?" I ask Elaine.

"Don't you know?" From Frannie's exaggerated tone of disbelief, you'd think I had asked if the earth was really round.

"She's new. She's temporary." Elaine explains to her puzzled friends. She turns back to me saying, "Everyone agreed not to talk to him, not to sit with him. It's called blackballing." Frannie nods at this explanation.

"But why?"

Frannie opens her mouth to answer, but she's not fast enough. Elaine's already answering. "He tried to get everyone to pray. Like at every meal. He told one woman that God wanted her to wear a dress to dinner, not pants. I tell you, no man but Richard will ever have the right to make an observation about what I should or should not wear. I mean, no other man. Period. This guy, he crosses the line. He crosses all kinds of lines. He reaches for other peoples' plates and then apologizes or cries. We hate when he cries, right?"

Elaine's friends nod in unison.

"Yes, I can see how all of that is annoying. But I'm curious: how did he react when people talked to him about changing his behavior?"

"Plenty of us got into fights with him, yelled at him. But he never made sense in return."

"I don't know, but it seems a bit harsh to cut him off that way. In the place where he's going to live for the rest of his life." I twist around involuntarily to look at Mr. Smyth, but he's left the dining room already.

Residents here lay down a sizeable chunk of money to buy their apartment, although the deal only lasts until they die. Every month they pay a not inconsiderable chunk of change that covers all sorts of services – from the van that drives you around to the nurse who is on duty downstairs. They buy a meal package – or they agree to a kind of ala carte arrangement where they pay by the meal. But that's very expensive. And when residents pass away, their heirs get back 80% of what they had plunked down originally to buy the place, which reverts back to the company.

"He's not the only one," Frannie says, pouting. "We're gonna be here forever, too."

"I don't think he is entirely well," I say, "but

then which of us doesn't have our complaints at this age."

Elaine ignores me, as if she hadn't protected her own confused husband. She scowls and a chill falls over the table. Ah-oh, I guess I'm the next in line to be banned. I flash back to the days of McCarthyism when anyone who defended people on the Blacklist soon joined them there. I mean it's not at all the same, but inside this little cosmos – some people almost never leave the walls of this building – the social norms seem pretty strict, and, in this case at least, the punishment is dire.

None of them responds for a full minute; they just throw looks over the cutlery to each other as if making a pact in secret body language. Then they resume their chatter, being careful to exclude me.

What to do? Apologize for speaking out of turn? Tell them to go fuck themselves? Reach for someone else's plate and then break out in wild sobs?

It feels so junior high that I just calmly finish my meal and leave the table without any further drama. I say a polite 'See you later" as I go. I wait in the drawing room for Sarah to be done eating – I've got to run this mess by her – but Sarah walks out with Hiba, Mia, and Jeanne, her scrabble partner who I haven't met yet. "It's not easy to find someone just that shade better than you to play scrabble with," she had told me. "Jeanne used to be a competitor – I've always been just a recreational player – so she really knows all the tricks. We call our daily game our brain calisthenics."

The three friends are deep in a conversation so Sarah just waves a greeting my way and continues on into the games room with them. Clearly this isn't a good time for sharing a moan with Sarah. But even that gesture, that wave, has turned me on. When it comes to Sarah, it doesn't take much. How old was I when I met Bernard and he could make me wet just from a glance? It was over 60 years ago. Amazing to return now to that state of desire.

As they disappear from sight, I only wish I could think of someone else to talk to. I haven't really made new friends yet, just Emmanuel, sort of. It's a sobering thought. I can't rely on Sarah alone if I'm going to build a new life in Manor House. I certainly don't want to be dependent on one person, most especially not on a lover. I figure that in senior housing, that's a losing strategy. Here today; taking a dirt nap, as a friend used to say, tomorrow.

The worst part of growing old is the shrinking of your circle. Your peers die – in fact they start doing that in their 60s and it never ends. Your family dies: in my immediate family both my husband and one son are long gone. In my birth family, I'm the last to remain standing. And as my mobility grows more restricted, I have fewer opportunities to get out and meet new folks. It's isolating to age.

I swivel around when I hear Emmanuel's voice. I realize that it's coming from the manager's office just down the hall. By twisting around, I can see Mr. Meade standing behind his desk, leaning heavily on his hands on the top of his desk, his head jutting forward toward Emmanuel. Henry Smyth is on the side of the desk, crying and pointing at Emmanuel, who is shaking his head with the most despondent look.

I can't figure out any legitimate way to get closer to hear what's going on, but it looks tense. What can I do? I don't have a role around here, not even that of a resident, so I can't exactly barge in. Emmanuel looks so unhappy; I want to be there for him. When Henry leaves, Mr. Meade sits back down. Emmanuel continues to stand and to speak with animation.

Finally Emmanuel leaves the manager's office and walks straight out the front door. He takes a few steps away from the entrance before he stops to breathe deeply. I give him a minute or two and then I follow him out and ask, "What the hell's going on, Emmanuel?"

I didn't mean to startle him, but he jumps before he sees that it's me. "Oh! So glad to see a friend. It is hard to explain. I am not sure myself. Mr. Smyth is missing a Jesus cross with jewels and he insists that I have taken it. Why would I want a cross of any sort? I am a Muslim. My parents are elders in Jamia Mosque of Nairobi. It makes no sense."

"Hold on a minute Emmanuel. Back up. Did you steal his cross?

Emmanuel's eyes open in consternation. "Most emphatically not."

"Exactly! No matter if you are Christian or you are Muslim, the important point is that you are not a thief. What was Henry's evidence? Did he give a reason to suspect you?"

"Lewanda says that in America it is enough to be Black to be suspicious."

"Yes, that's often true. But did Henry say he saw you take it?"

"No, he demanded that Mr. Meade have the police search my room."

"What did Mr. Meade say?"

"He asked me not to go in any more residents' rooms until he got to the bottom of it. I am very unhappy with that decision. If I cannot go into the rooms, I cannot help the people, so I will not keep my job."

"What a shitty situation." People are coming outside and I want to keep talking. "Let's sit in the garden," I say. We walk to a bench behind some hedges that give it privacy and sit down. "Funny enough," I tell him, "today I made people mad when I asked why they excluded Henry from everything. All the residents dislike him and they all agreed not to talk to him. He must be a very frustrated man, besides being difficult."

"It is a good word for him," Emmanuel says. "Difficult. I tried to help him with some things but he is always rude. He wanted me to pray Christian prayers with him and I told him I could not. He asked me to go on my knees and I told him I would not. And that was only yesterday."

"Did you tell Mr. Meade that?"

"No. Not with Mr. Smyth in the office."

"Did you ever see a cross with jewels? Did anyone ever see it? I think *his* room should be searched first."

"Whose room should be searched?" We had not heard Sarah's approach across the grass to the bench where we are sitting. Emmanuel jumps up, saying "Excuse me," nods to me, and goes inside.

Sarah sits down in his place. "You look a bit ragged."

"Have I got stories for *you*!"

9. The Moochers Arrive

"Does your family know about us?" Sarah asks, as we sit in the sunny courtyard waiting for Michael and his brood to arrive.

"My family has not forgiven me for refusing to give up my life to serve theirs. Not one of them has asked me how I am or what I'm doing or how it is here. They've just bitched, bitched, bitched that I'm a failure as a grandmother."

"How'd they all end up living in your house in the first place? When I met you, you were living alone."

"Michael and Emily made a number of dumb decisions and both ended up unemployed. They have three kids, the youngest one adopted from China after there was no longer any household income. The timing sucked. I had just visited here at Manor House and had decided to sell my place and move in – remember that day?"

Sarah nods, saying, "You mean the day you sat with the saleswoman in the office and figured it all out? What a happy day that was for me!"

"Me too, but not for long. I got home, wiped out but pretty euphoric. I was walking around looking at all the junk I've acquired, thinking: *That's* got to go. Wonder if I can sell *that*. Maybe the kids want *that*. Then the doorbell rings and Michael and Emily have landed on my doorstop. So I only had a couple of hours to enjoy the idea of dumping that big pile of stones and coming here, where you and Freda and Lenny were, before Mr. Doom and Mrs. Gloom arrived to tell me otherwise."

"How did they put it? How did they ask such a huge favor?"

"They thought they were doing a good deed. I believe they sincerely figured it was a win-win. They're completely oblivious about me – mainly because they're so taken up with the stresses of their own lives that they never stop to actually ask me anything. They just make assumptions. The worst part of it was that they not only wanted my house: they wanted my time and energy, too. I guess they swallowed all the Hallmark messages about grandmothers just dying to babysit. Because once they all descended on my house, they more or less dumped the kids on me. I think they assumed my life was one big blank and that they were showing me a big kindness. Meanwhile, I was busy dreaming about you" – and I lean over and kiss Sarah's cheek – "while they were congratulating themselves on keeping me occupied."

"So they don't have a clue."

"They're not interested."

"And how are we going to play this?"

"As casually as possible. Frankly, I think they might have a problem with me dating someone after all these years."

"*Someone*? I think you're being a bit naïve, yourself. What about the fact that I'm a woman, a lesbian? Even *you* aren't comfortable with the term, let alone your family."

"Well, Michael *is* my son. I can't imagine that that aspect of it would be a big deal."

Sarah shakes her head. "Listen, Lillian. I don't know Michael and Emily, but I've been the brunt of a shitload of hatred in my life because of loving women. Decades of it. So I'm pretty mistrustful . We probably should've talked about this long before your family was on its way. Let's be serious. You've lived 84 years in a pretty conventional way. You were married. You had a couple of kids. You're white. You're educated. It's not that you haven't had your share of tragedy and loss; it's just that you've never been an outsider. I worry that you don't realize that 'dating,' as you put it, isn't quite so acceptable when it's with another old woman."

"In my heart, I'm feeling a bit defensive. But in my brain, I know that you're right, Sarah. I've never had any gay people as close friends, but I've read a lot – Audre Lorde, for example." I can hear how lame this sounds. "Bernard and I were very close to another couple from his work, a Black couple, although I've lost touch with them now. The wife once said a similar thing to me, something I'll never forget. She said I had no idea the layers of dark attitudes she had to fight through to get to a little sunlight."

Sarah smiles. "Yeah, I understand her. It's tough to wade through peoples' misconceptions and fantasies and…"

"There they are," I jump up and point to a brown SUV parking in the lot. A member of my family pops out from every door. I try to see them with Sarah's eyes, a stranger's eyes. Michael is slouch-shouldered and, good grief, he's already nearly bald. Emily is disheveled in her usual Mother Earth style. She's wearing the same shapeless floral dress and Mary Jane shoes that she always wears. I used to think her lack of style was part of her charm. She's clutching Lee to her hip, but the toddler is squirming to get free. Leon sulks and hangs back. Has he changed so much or did I just fail to see how awkward he looks? He seems to have sprouted from the feet up. His tennis shoes are as big as a couple of rowboats, his legs like crooked stilts, and his face overwhelmed with pimples. Ah, but there's Lisa, smiling and composed, a lovely junior high schooler. She catches my eye, thrilled to see me.

"Bubbe!" Lisa calls, walking faster and looking happier than the rest of the crew. "Isn't it beautiful here!" She hugs me and whispers, "Do the other old people here swear like you do?"

Emily comes forward and thrusts Lee into my arms, almost knocking me off balance. He is sucking a pacifier that is dribbling spit. He wraps his arms around my head and nuzzles my ear, tickling me. I cry out, "Lee! My ear!" – giggling. Oh dear me, this toddler is giving me flashbacks to the other night when Sarah licked around my ear. I turn my head to lock eyes with her. She smiles and seems to understand. I give the baby a peck on the cheek and a squeeze before pushing him right back into Emily's hands. Sarah pulls her red railroad hankie out of the back pocket of her jeans and gives it to me. I dry off Lee's drippings and return the hankie, accompanied by a glance I hope is full of my appreciation for her making me feel so looked after.

Finally Michael approaches and gives me an air-kiss from a foot away. "Mom."

A clumsy silence falls. I see that Leon is still lingering near the car. "Hi, Leon." He tips his head, not really making eye contact.

"Everyone, I want you to meet Sarah." Michael and Emily mumble some kind of acknowledgement. "She's one of the main reasons I came to Manor House." More mumbles. Lisa still has her arm around me.

Oh! They aren't really that interested. They're hardly paying attention. Except, that is, Lisa. What a sweetie! She approaches Sarah, takes up both her hands, and says, "Any friend of Bubbe's is a friend of mine." Now that she's shown the adults how to behave, Emily wiggles the baby at Sarah and Michael finally walks over to shake her hand. "Nice to meet you." Although they may remember that I had said that one of the attractions of Manor House was a romantic attachment, I now realize that it may never have occurred to them that the person was a woman. Sarah. Michael and Emily didn't get it. But then they didn't get much this past year, understandably distracted as they are with the loss of jobs, the addition of Lee to their family, and their forced move into my house.

They settle on the benches of a picnic table in the courtyard. "We'll go into lunch in about a quarter of an hour," I tell them. "So fill me in."

"If you really want to know," Michael says, already whining, "things are worse than we thought with that start-up." Michael had given up a brilliant engineering career with a Fortune 500 company to buy into the fantasy of some dodgy start-up that paid him half his salary in shares. The founders had convinced him that the shares would be valuable one day – that whole Amazon-like fairy tale. Until, that is, the CFO walked out with the bank account in his back pocket – well, his back pocket was apparently in Switzerland. The company collapsed – it turned out the CFO hadn't been paying the bills. The shares were worthless and Michael was out of a job just as the recession hit and Lee came into the family.

"What could be worse?"

"Turns out that I had enough shares on paper that I might be in the group that's liable for the debts they incurred."

I instantly translated what he said, because what he really means is, "We're really poor and we're going to suck up every cent you have, Mom. And we're going to keep squatting in your house."

"Have your networking sessions led to any job prospects?"

"The situation is pretty awful out there. I've been writing people to ask for informational meetings and then once we get together that person has either lost his job or feels he's about to. In fact, engineers who used to make a couple hundred thousand are now working as bookkeepers and things like that. Or they're planning to go back to school to change careers – like to teach or something."

"What about taking any old job, even if it's low wage and not with computers? Some income would be better than none."

"What d'ya mean, Mum? You mean work at McDonalds? How would I ever find a job then? I'd get stuck, since I'd have to work 100 hours a week to make even a quarter of what I was making."

Michael's point is well taken. I look into his eyes and say, "Well, I can certainly see what you're saying. I just hope you'll be as flexible as possible, because you never know what might pop up. I wish you the best of luck."

My reaction isn't what he's hoping for. He looks at Emily, who purses her lips, before turning and saying to her shoes. "Yeah, thanks." This is how it works: I'm squeezed between the consequences of these start-up losers on one side and my family's very real-life crisis on the other – and all of it is threatening my last dreams, my last years, my last affair. When I tell Freda about this later, she says, "Yes, darlink, they're stopping Lillian's last affair. Vhich sounds like the name of a tragic novel."

Meanwhile, the kids are looking back and forth trying to make sense of what's going on. I can feel Sarah at my side, looking at me. I'm daydreaming and a gloomy mood is settling over my dining guests. I've got to deflect everyone's frustration. Not for nothing am I a culinary Jew. It's time to turn to the food. "Hey, why don't we go in. We've had a big table reserved for the family."

Four adults and three kids crowd around a table meant for six and look over the menu. "So you live here too?" Emily asks Sarah, once we're settled.

"Yes, I've lived here for several years. I'm friends with Freda, and so is Lillian. That's how we met."

"Who's Freda, Bubbe?"

"You know Freda and her brother Lenny, Lisa."

"The ones with the accent?"

"The ones who made you those sugar cookies you loved, honey."

"Oh yeah," Leon says. "With the colored sugars on them. Hey, they were great. So do Freda and Lenny live here?"

Aargh. Do any of them pay any attention at all to what I tell them? "Remember how I got to come here for six weeks? Because Freda and Lenny went to take care of their cousin in Florida and I'm staying in Freda's empty apartment."

"Why didn't you stay at home if your friends are gone anyway?"

"Lisa, I don't want to live in a big house with stairs anymore. I want to sell it and buy a place here."

Lisa stares at Sarah with a warm curiosity.

"And that's not all," I continue. "I want to get to know Sarah better. Much, much better."

Michael had been drifting, listless, probably disappointed that his mommy hadn't come up with instant solutions to all his problems. But now he twitches. At last I have his attention. He screws up his brow and exchanges one of those very obvious 'secret' glances with Emily, who takes a breath and speaks up.

"Mother, not in front of the children."

"What?"

"Let's keep private things private."

"So we shouldn't," Sarah intervenes, "tell the kids that you and Michael are married?"

"I wasn't talking to you."

"But you are now. And hopefully you will be for a long time to come." She puts her hand over mine. I flash on one of Freda's sayings: 'A good friend is better than a bad relative.'

Lewanda comes up to the table to take our orders. The children can't make up their minds. They're worse than the old people. In the end, both teenagers order mac 'n cheese. Oy. But maybe they're flummoxed by the situation.

Before the food even comes, Emily starts to cry. Lee, who's sitting on her lap, joins in. Leon's bewildered. "What's going on?" Lisa gets it, but she doesn't know what to do. I make a mental note: Lisa's going to be an obsessive problem-solver after growing up with parents who are useless under stress.

At first Michael locks eyes with me and shrugs, as if to say, I live with this stuff all the time.

Emily catches the look and says, "Michael!" She's scolding him for not – in her mind – standing up for her. Against what, lord only knows. To defend her small-mindedness?

He in turn gives Sarah a resentful glance, saying. "Look what you've done!"

I'm not having it. "Michael! Shut the fuck up."

Emily scrapes her chair back, hefts Lee over her

shoulder, yells to the kids, "Come on. We're going," and runs out of the dining room. Every person at every table in the dining room is staring our way. Lisa stands but doesn't want to go. She seems devastated. Michael stands up slowly, taking her hand, and softly says. "If you think you're ever going to get us out of the house, Mother, you've got another thing coming. I'm not paying for your perversions."

"As far as I can see," I answer, "you're not paying for jack shit."

10. The Pressure Builds

Later that evening I leave the apartment for dinner; but as I pull the door shut, I realize that I can't lock it because I've left the keys inside on the sideboard. I go back in and decide that I might as well have a prophylactic pee, to forestall interrupting my meal. Afterwards, when I pull the door shut, I remember, oh dear, I never did pick up the keys, so I return to grab them. Good thing they designed the doors so that you need to use the key to lock up. The only good thing about a declining memory is that it makes me do a lot more walking than I would otherwise. I finally make it to the elevator. As I exit on the ground floor, Emmanuel waylays me.

"What's happening?" I ask him. "I haven't seen you since those horrible accusations."

"Mr. Meade gave me other kinds of work to do, the kinds of work that are not involving the residents. In the storeroom, making things neat, and that type of thing. This morning I asked him what was planned. And I took your advice. I reminded him that I am not a Christian. I told him about Henry Smyth's anger when I would not get down on my knees to pray."

"How did he react?"

"He put his face in his hands," Emmanuel says, "and admitted that I was not the first non-Christian to tell him such a thing. But that Mr. Smyth had not accused anyone else of a crime. He said that he restricted me because he didn't want Mr. Smyth to take the issue to the police. He had promised Mr. Smyth that he would look into it himself."

"Would it help if I wrote a letter to Mr. Meade about what an asset you are to Manor House, how valuable you have been to me?"

Emmanuel almost smiles, but not quite. "I have no idea how they are doing these things in this country. And I do not want to impose on your goodness."

The nearby doors of the elevator open and, among others, Henry Smyth comes out. When he sees me and Emmanuel, he stomps over, screaming. "A homo and a thief! Plotting your heathen plots. I should have known you two were in cahoots."

Emmanuel can't quite understand what Smyth is saying, but I understand only too well. His words and hostility explode like a cannon ball in my face. A homo? He called me a homo! Emmanuel is standing slightly behind me, frozen. Somewhere in my mind is a reminder that this is worse for Emmanuel, whose job hangs in the balance, and I should do something. But all I want to do is cry. And I sure the hell am not going to do that.

I'm a bundle of conflicts. I don't even consider myself gay – or haven't ever done so for the past 84 years. But it's none of his fucking business and this insult is wider than just me. Imagine if he had screamed at Sarah.

Meanwhile, poor Emmanuel. Spending all this time keeping a low profile in the stock rooms, and the first time he peeks out in public, he is assaulted by this fundamentalist freak. I want to open my mouth and release the sewer of "fuck yous" that I keep dammed up right behind my tongue, but I've got to think about Emmanuel.

I notice a sparkle and realize that Elaine and Mimi must've come out of the elevator at the same time as Henry and they're standing on the side. Before my heart has time to sink, Elaine walks up at full speed, shaking her fist at Henry Smyth. "You again!" she hisses, "you've been so rude to so many people in this residence that I believe you were planted here by the competition."

Lewanda, hearing the commotion from the dining room, has now turned up and stands beside Emmanuel defiantly. Mimi takes heart from the number of people surrounding Henry, and she and her sequins step up as well. "And you wonder why no one will sit with you, you repulsive toad." With a triumphant glance she looks towards Elaine for approval.

Lewanda takes Emmanuel's arm and quietly draws him away. I nod yes, yes, to Lewanda, so she hustles her friend faster through the kitchen door – just in time to be out of sight when Mr. Meade turns up.

"What's going on here?"

Elaine wants center stage. "It's Henry Smyth again, sir. He's throwing around accusations and insults and all manner of slurs. If my Richard were still with us, he wouldn't stand for it. That's just how he was. He would object. He would be pounding on your door, Mr. Meade. He would be demanding that a certain level of decorum – you remember he always used to say that? – a certain level of decorum should be maintained. What are you going to do about Henry? This is the umpteenth time he's disrupted Manor House with his rudeness, now isn't it?" This last question she addresses to the rest of us.

"Yes, it is. It certainly is," says Mimi, looking around encouragingly. I mumble assent.

Other people are gathering, all talking at once. It seems that each one has suffered Smyth's verbal poison. Not a few complain of his aggressive religiosity. "Smyth threatened me with damnation because I was stepping out with more than one woman in Manor House," grumbles one old man with a reputation as a Don Juan. "It's got nothing to do with him and in fact he confused my neighbor with my girlfriend."

"He told me I was immodest," Mimi says, not to be outdone, "that I didn't dress right for a matron of my age. He called me a matron!" Others pipe up as well and things become so heated that Mr. Meade asks Mr. Smyth to join him, alone, in the office.

I'm glad that in the ruckus, the slights to me and to Emmanuel have been more or less forgotten, while everyone else rushed to testify. This is good. Mr. Meade has just been inundated with a pile of evidence of this resident's chronic rudeness. I'll give this to Henry: he senses very accurately where each individual's most tender button is buried; he gets each of us where it hurts the most. I'm glad Mr. Meade doesn't know it all started with an attack on Emmanuel and me. As we say in my Tribe, this could eventually be good for the Jews.

As the early diners are leaving and the later ones are arriving, the crowd grows. Elaine, in the middle of it, is in her glory, quoting her dead husband and ramping up the froth. Folks see the hubbub and ask, "What happened?" "What's going on?" The bitch session about Henry Smyth is turning into a bit of an old age lynch mob, and I'm uncomfortable with all the vitriol. With the timing of an experienced demagogue, Elaine cries, "Let's go to the manager's office, all of us. Let's ask him to get rid of Henry."

Oy! I'm always up for a righteous protest; but even a lying, arrogant fanatic shouldn't get thrown out of his housing. I hang back as about half of them surge down the hall towards the administrative offices. Fuck it. To hell with dinner. I'll nuke a baked potato and binge on fruit in my room. Maybe

I'll have a magic brownie to get the taste of Michael and Emily and Henry Smyth out of my mouth. How could all this happen in a single day?

An hour later my phone finally rings. Yikes! I've got to get the audio level of this phone turned down. It's a damned assault each time it rings. Sarah is booming out at me; I hold the receiver away from my ear. "I didn't see you in the dining room. It's mayhem down there. Do you know what's going on?"

I surprise myself by breaking into tears.

"Lillian? What's wrong? I'm coming right up to your apartment."

I'm really not ready to talk about all of this with Sarah. I need to sort this tumultuous day out. But a few minutes later she's sitting on my couch as I pace the room with my uneven gait, sniffling and dabbing a hankie at my bodily fluids.

"Sit here," Sarah pats the seat next to her. "And I'll hold you while you fill me in."

"No, I'll sit across from you, where I won't have to twist to see you. I guess we should talk."

I pour a couple of glasses of lemonade in the kitchen, wheel them into the living room, and place them on the coffee table between us. My breath is still a little jumpy from crying, but I recognize that I'm feeling calmer, just having Sarah here with me. "It's bad enough that I've had my first taste of gay bashing, or whatever it's called. But, shit, did I have to get slapped with a double dose? First Michael and Emily – I could've choked them. And then that fundie creep Henry called me a 'homo' and said I was perverted down in the lobby. And there's another thing, Sarah, it's about you. The way you keep talking about being a lesbian. Lesbian this. Lesbian that. Can't we just be two people who love each other?" I stop to control myself, taking a big breath in the hopes of avoiding yet another cry. "It's all a bit much."

I do credit Sarah. Instead of going on the defensive over my last comment, she is all sympathy. "Oh no! I had no idea about Henry insulting you. You'll have to tell me about it. And it was terrible with Michael and Emily, but I did try to warn you that it might take them a while to adjust to your new way of living. She reaches across for both my hands and holds them, staring right into my eyes. "I'm sorry, Lillian, that so much got dumped on you all at once. And I congratulate you for holding it together so well. Today's really been an overload of trouble. But you have to understand about me. I *am* a lesbian, and have been since high school, you know, in the 50s when people were still put away or given shock treatments. I know it's not your identity – at least not yet" – we both smile – "but it *is* mine."

"Yes, I understand that. Or just a bit of it. Did you know that you were a lesbian when you were in high school?"

"We didn't have those kinds of words, back then. The idea of 'coming out' or of identifying with one sexuality or another, that didn't happen until the start of the 70s. No, if you had feelings for another woman, and I did, especially if you acted on those feelings, and I did, then you were a pervert, a sicko, a nasty queer. It was all negative and beyond the pale. It was dangerous, illegal. We stayed hidden."

"The truth is, Sarah, that I'm only now, since I met you, facing how easy my life has been – except for Norman dying of course. But I met Bernard, married him, and everyone praised us and bought us pans and silverware. Your life with all that secrecy and fear, it's another universe. And, I don't know how to say this, but it's all a bit much for me. I'm feeling buried under conflicts and problems. So much has been going on. First, my kids' forcibly take over my house. Then I move here to Peyton Place. And now I'm getting attacked by my family and by strangers too. Plus, all of this is happening in the middle of all the emotional turmoil of my romantic feelings for you. Just reciting this list is exhausting. Maybe I'm just too old. I don't think I'm up for becoming a target at this stage of my life."

"What are you saying?"

"I don't even know what I'm trying to say. I'm

not sure what I'm feeling – other than overwhelmed. But perhaps we need to put a hold on us. I've lived through 84 years without being called a pervert. It's not how I pictured my last decade."

All of a sudden I need to pee. Sarah and I have been leaning forward clutching both hands across the table. I stand up. "Gotta pee. Be right back." It's bad timing, but there's nothing I can do about it. Sighing, Sarah falls back deep into the cushions of the couch. "I'm sorry, Sarah."

As soon as I sit on the toilet I realize that I've been holding it in for a long time. Oy. At least I get this short break. I feel like my life is hanging on the brink of things I never anticipated: on the brink of a big love; on the brink of disaster. Do I need all this tumult at this point in my life? How I wish I could stop and call Freda. I could use a consultation with her right now. But I stand and flush, stopping to splash my face with cold water before returning to the living room.

"Do you want some more lemonade?" I ask Sarah. She looks at me strangely and then I see that her glass is still full. I'm on autopilot, and stalling.

"No, I want to know what you were about to say. And I want it straight, as it were. Are you breaking up with me before we're even truly together?"

I'm taken aback. "That's strong language, damn it. I don't think that's what I'm saying at all. I just need a breather. I'm just not certain. So much is going on that I'm feeling flooded by it all. I'm just asking for a time-out so that I can think."

Sarah's face is a transparent window into her heart. I watch as shock, pain, and then anger cycles across her face.

"You know, my friends told me I was crazy to get involved with a straight woman."

"That's not fair!"

"I agree. This isn't fair."

Sarah leans down to grab her backpack and then stands up. I jump up, too. "Wait, don't leave. Not like this. Let's talk."

"We'll talk another time. Your day has been horrible and my day has just become a bummer. Sorry, but I've got to get out of here."

She walks with strong resolve to the door and goes out without a backward look.

I stare at the door which has closed behind her until my leg twitches, reminding me that I'm standing still in the middle of the living room.

11. Naked at Last

First thing this morning I check my refrigerator. What a relief to find a yogurt whose sell-by date isn't until tomorrow, milk that didn't yet reek of sour, and a French roll in a bag in the freezer. How great to make my own breakfast – anything to avoid the drama of the dining hall.

The phone rings. It's 8:00 sharp. "Mother?" That one annoying word blasts out on the steroids of the hyped-up phone speaker. Why does Emily insist on calling me "mother" when I've suggested endlessly that my name is Lillian and that I'm not really Emily's mother. My feeling is that I've got one live child and one dead child, and with that I'm done being a mother.

"Yes, Emily. Good morning."

"We were very upset – well, the children in particular were – by how our meal ended yesterday."

Wait, was Emily going to apologize? That would be a first.

"If only you hadn't invited that stranger to join us, it would've been such a nice visit."

"By stranger you mean Sarah?"

"Yes."

"She's not a stranger to me. It was my invite, my table. Don't you think I can invite anyone I want?"

"Oh, I'm sure she's very nice. I'm just thinking of the children. They're at such impressionable ages, so vulnerable. I worry about them."

And that's about all you do for them, I almost say aloud. Emily and Michael adopted Lee about the same time as they descended on my home, miles from their own neighborhood. They ripped Lisa away from her first boyfriend and Leon away from his first baseball team and then proceeded to ignore them. Emily was all gooey over the new child, who rarely left her arms, and Michael was either watching a game or off on one of his non-productive networking sessions. Neither of them was working and neither of them was looking after the older kids. When I was still home, that had fallen into my lap. Now that I'm at Manor House, I'm afraid my grandchildren may be feeling lost.

"Why do you have to worry about Sarah and the kids?"

"Um, you know."

"No, I don't know."

"It's just not really a lifestyle that Michael and I want to expose the kids to at this point."

"Emily, even though you are a young woman, your brain somehow got stuck in the 1950s. Listen, it's early in the morning. Do you have a reason for calling?"

"Yes, Michael and I talked it over last night. We want you to come back home. Either that, or sign the house over to us, now that this stranger is more important to you than your own flesh and blood."

"Would it be mean to remind you that I share neither flesh nor blood with you, Emily? And as to the suggestion that I give you my house, would it be rude to say Fuck You? After this conversation, I'm considering changing my will and leaving everything to the gay liberation movement. Goodbye."

I hang up the phone deliberately, seething. The nerve! I grab the receiver again to call Sarah, and then I remember the disastrous conversation from last night. My hand hovers and then I replace the handset.

I'm making a mess of things.

Someone knocks on the door. What now?

Emmanuel. "Excuse me for bothering you…"

"Your visit is never a bother. Would you like to come in?"

"I'm not allowed to, no thank you. I just did not see you at breakfast and I was wanting to tell you of my discussion with the manager. He asked me, as a favor, to keep doing the work I am doing because they are trying to find a way to remove Mr. Henry Smyth from Manor House. But that I was not to tell anyone. However, I did want to tell you."

While he speaks, Emmanuel looks from left to right to make sure he's not being overheard.

"Then your job is not in jeopardy?"

"Jeopardy?"

"At risk."

"No. He said he was satisfied with my work."

"I am so glad." We shake hands. It's the first good news in a while and I want to hug him. After all, in some ways Emmanuel is my only disinterested friend in Manor House. But I decide it's not a great idea and make do with smiles and shakes.

"And I brought you a present." He thrusts a little box into my hands. "You said you liked Kenyan tea, and this is tea I received from my sisters who sent me a box of things from back home."

"Your sisters? How many do you have?"

"I have three in Nairobi and one in Philadelphia."

"In Philly? How long as she been here?"

"She's older than the rest of us. She was born of my father's first wife. After he lost his wife, he married our mother and we were born. She came to the United States to study to be a dentist, and then she married an American dentist and stayed. She is the one who brought me here in the first place."

"But you didn't go to Philly."

"No, I didn't. I got a job here and for the time being, until I can save money, I will be here. My sister's husband owns a property here and so I have a two-room apartment from him for a low price. That's why I live here."

I lean against the doorjamb. I don't mind walking and I don't mind sitting, but I find it hard to stand in one place very long. "Please, come inside and I'll put on the kettle." He slips in, saying, "Sorry, no times for drinking tea right now." I shake the package at him.

"How great is this! I haven't had Kenyan tea since that time I bought some at Duty Free in the Nairobi Airport. Did I tell you about that? Should I?" Emmanuel's face lights up. "Yes, please." I wonder how lonely he is, how often he gets to chat with a friend.

"So when I got to the Duty-Free section, I was surprised to find a bunch of stalls instead of stores, like I was used to. A tea farmer sat at a folding table that he had piled with big plastic bags stuffed with tea. He wanted $4 for a bag and so I bought two bags and gave him $10. On the airplane, they didn't have room for the two big bags of tea. I actually held one on my lap the whole trip back while a particularly kind tea-loving stewardess stowed the other in the cabinet where the bathroom supplies are kept. There were too many jokes about it being pot..."

Emmanuel was following me easily until the word "pot," which he did not recognize. "Uh, do you know the word weed? Marijuana?" He did not. I begin to play-act, smoking a joint, rolling my eyes, lolling my head.

"Ah, you mean *bangi*. Our word in Swahili, it's *bangi*."

"Yes, well on the plane they teased me about bringing *bangi* – am I pronouncing it right? – to America. The customs people were not so amused. They eventually let me through. At home I made small individual sacks of Kenyan tea and passed them out to all my friends and they all loved it."

Emmanuel is getting increasingly nervous, looking around. "I am pleased for my country," he says, distracted, "but I think I must return to my office of work."

I've been babbling. I've held him up. All he wanted to do was bring me up-to-date, give me the gift, and get back to his job. He was just being courteous, showing gratitude. It had been the wrong time to drone on about my whole tea saga. He was stressed about hanging onto his job, but had run up to fill me in. He's so generous and I'm running at the mouth. I'm turning into what Freda would call a *kibitzer*, what Lisa would call a Chatty Cathy. Emmanuel, meanwhile, has gone out the door and is flying down the hall. What's wrong with me? Am I losing my ability to read situations? I sure to hell seem to be in a period of screwing everything up.

I go back inside. My breakfast things are still on the table, uneaten. I put on the kettle, fill the tea bulb, and steam myself a delicious cup of Kenyan black tea.

The truth? I'm feeling lost. This was all supposed to be a new chapter in my life. Instead it's a bunch of *mishugas*, as Freda would say, craziness. I know damned well that I don't have the time or the energy to waste on little hassles, but I still haven't figured out how to avoid them. Over my second cup of tea, I force myself to get a grip on my priorities.

I need to sort out what's important – no, it's all important: Michael, Emmanuel, the house, Sarah – I guess I have to figure out how I want to live my life. And then figure out the order of things I've got to tidy up. The minute I put my mind to making a list, I know instantly what's at the top of it. Or rather who's at the top. Sarah. Sarah's the One. It's time to get my butt in gear, to remember why I volunteered for all this change. Because somewhere buried in the temporary chaos is a chance for love. Love! It never occurred to me that I would want a lover again. And certainly not that I would actually *get* a lover at this, the last stage of my life.

I drain my cup and call, but Sarah doesn't answer. So I leave a message saying I'm sure if we get together we can get over this hiccup. Oy! Will the word "hiccup" sound too dismissive? Should I call back? I stop myself.

I'm impatient so a few minutes later I try her cell.

"Hello," Sarah says. "How are you?"

"I've had my tea and I'm desperate to see you."

She doesn't say anything.

"Where are you? I tried your apartment."

"I'm in the back garden, alone with my journal, jotting down some thoughts. I had breakfast with Hiba and she helped me sort out my feelings."

"Can you be interrupted?"

"Apparently so. I just have been."

Silence again.

"This is so awkward, Sarah, but I just know that if you come around I could change the vibe with just one cup of this Kenyan tea Emmanuel gave me."

Silence.

"Please?"

I can just picture Sarah, out in the back garden, probably in well-washed jeans and a large button-down Oxford shirt over them. She'll be in her sandals. Perhaps she's even using the jeweled bands to fasten her pigtails. My heart's thumping with anxiety at the length of this silence.

"I want you so much, Sarah, and that's the truth."

"That's good to hear, because that certainly wasn't clear yesterday."

"Please, let's not do this on the phone. I'll put the kettle on."

Sarah hesitates. "Okay. I'm on my way."

Oh Jesus. Look at my living room! I grab the

most prominent piles of discarded clothes and stuff them into the coat closet. On the way to the kitchen I trip – I'm not totally accustomed to Freda's place yet – and stub my toe on my own cane, which I have left leaning against the wall. I hold onto the doorjamb and shake my foot, which is tingling anyway from the neuropathy. I grit my teeth, put on the kettle, drop a few store-bought cookies onto a little plate, and barely set up a tray with a milk boat and sugar bowl when Sarah knocks on the door.

When I open the door, I feel such a rush of desire that I wrap myself around Sarah's tall, strong frame and hug her. She shuffles inside, dragging me along, and kicks the door shut, leaning back against it for support. I nuzzle into her collarbone and feel like I never want to relinquish her again.

She peels me away with a smile. "I thought I was coming over to talk things through. And wasn't there a rumor of Kenyan tea?"

She shrugs off her denim jacket and then seats herself on the couch. The kettle shouts for my attention. As I go into the kitchenette to turn it off and pour it into the teapot, Sarah asks me, "Why are you limping so much?"

"I'll explain later. We have more important things to discuss right now."

Walking without my cane, I return with the wheeled tray-table. She hasn't taken her eyes off of me – not like she's cruising me; more like she's scrutinizing me. Confusion infuses her expression.

I sit across from her and when I pick up the teapot, I realize that I've forgotten cups. I start to get up, but Sarah is already on her way to the kitchen to grab two out of the cupboard. Once we each cradle a cup of hot tea, I try to explain what I don't understand myself. "I may not be a militant like you, but I've sure as hell had a mini-revolution in my personal life. I'm sorry I'm not a lesbian, at least not an experienced one. But I'm 84. I've been single for many years, and suddenly all I can think about is hootchie cootchie with the most attractive librarian on earth. It's a god-damned miracle and it's got me in and out of sorts, as they say."

I stop to take a breath and Sarah nods for me to continue. "My daughter-in-law called first thing this morning to piss me off. She and Michael 'decided' that I should sign the house over to them. I told her I had decided to change my will and leave it to the gay liberation movement."

Sarah cracks up. "Be careful they don't try to take you to court as mentally incompetent!"

I giggle. "Fat chance."

"Don't be so sure. It happened to a friend of mine, Louise, a few years older than me. She was always a bit goofy and when her long-time partner died, she got goofier, took up mime lessons and posed nude at an art school. She hooked up with a much younger woman, in her 40s I guess, who had two little girls in elementary school. Louise moved them all right in, just as her son was hoping to stick her in assisted living and take over the family home. Louise was having the time of her life. She lavished her new girlfriend and the kids with all sorts of presents and trips. The downside was that Louise had had breast cancer three times, had a double mastectomy, and never really recovered from all the chemo and radiology. But you know what? I hung out with them a few times and that young woman, whatever-her-name was, was crazy about her, she really was. So were those little girls. The house was full of good vibes.

"Well, the next thing you know, her daughter and granddaughter, a pair of real assholes, blow the whistle on her. A social worker turns up and there are court papers and a very stressful mess, but, bless her, the girlfriend is on the case. She was a member of some lesbian group and they found Louise an advocate specializing in elder abuse who knew her way around the courts. It took some hearings and some meetings with a therapist, but in the end the judge ruled for Louise."

I love happy endings, "Jesus, I don't think Michael and Emily would ever take it that far, but if I catch your meaning, you know someone who knows someone who will take care of it for me, right? And how're Louise and her crew doing now?"

"Oh, Louise is dead. Long dead. She only had about 18 months with that little family – a big hunk of that wasted on fighting the daughter – but she did leave her girlfriend and the kids the house. That must be why I started telling you this whole long story."

I get up from my chair and limp around the coffee table to snuggle up to Sarah on the couch. "I'm sorry that I bungled yesterday so badly, but today I'm very clear. Your friend Louise was more on the ball than me. She knew it's now or never. As I said to Freda after I fell for you: If I'm going to go after one more affair of the heart at 84, I'd better get my ass in gear. I just know you're the one for me. I knew it once before, with Bernard, and I was right. I don't have any doubts: I just have a lack of skills."

"Skills?"

"Like this." I lay my hand over Sarah's breast. It's soft, small, loose, like a balloon that has only been blown up a little. At first I feel awkward cupping Sarah's breast, until, that is, I feel her pressing her chest against my hand. She likes it! I squeeze harder and she leans into me more.

I let go of that breast to reach for the other – already I feel more confident and excited. Sarah rotates her upper body, giving me a firmer grip. I shift to the edge of the couch so that I can use both hands. Suddenly I make a mental connection: No bra! She doesn't wear bras. That's the point of these oversized shirts! For some reason this seems downright liberated and I pinch each of her nipples, which I miraculously find on the first try. Sarah exhales with a shiver and whispers, "Oh yes."

For the first time in my life, I'm getting my own sexual buzz out of turning someone else on. For the first time I'm initiating, I'm taking the sexual lead, and, best of all, Sarah is digging it as much as I am.

From sitting this way, my leg is aching, so I stand up and so does Sarah. We walk hand-in-hand to my bedroom. Oy! I never did make my bed. Not a big deal. Not now. Sarah stands on one side and removes her shoes and slacks, leaving on her big shirt. I strip on the other side, my back to her, and then slip into my satin robe while holding on to a bureau for balance. Sarah plumps up all three pillows and stacks them against the headboard. "Come on," she says. I kick off my slippers and mount the stool I use to get onto the bed safely and sit with my back against the pillows. As I settle in, Sarah crawls in between my legs. She kneels up and pulls her shirt over her head. In the light of day I get to stare at those sweet breasts.

I have never seen another old woman's breasts. This is amazing. But wait. No, that's not true. I saw my mother's and those of her sister, my aunt, when I cared for them, before they died, my aunt shortly after my mom. I saw Freda half naked when we went to Cape Cod a few summers ago and shared a hotel room. When I think about it, I've seen lots of breasts, but this is the first time I'm looking with lust and longing. I never before felt what I feel now: that boobs are such a fetching sex organ.

Sarah takes my ankle and bends my leg, putting my foot flat on the bed. She repeats this with my other leg. Any sense of control, of my initiating the action has evaporated. I am, as they say, putty in her hands. What beautiful hands she has. These too are sex organs. I fixate on them, hoping they will touch me in intimate places. I lift my hands towards her face, caress her cheeks, and then pull her head down for a kiss on her mouth. Several kisses, including a quick visit by her tongue to my ear, making me giggle.

She sits back up on her heels. Her nipples are hard, the skin around them wrinkled. I pinch them again and Sarah throws her head back in surprise and pleasure. She reaches down and opens my robe, smiling, drinking in the view.

When I was in my late 60s, I was disappointed with my sagging breasts. By the time I was 75 I no longer gave a damn. I watch Sarah's face as she looks me over with delight and I can't really imagine what thrills her. My breasts are large and flattened out with age. They hang nearly to my lap when I'm sitting. Now that I am lounging, they fall to the sides of my ribcage. But looking down at myself, I see that my nipples are perky and my areolas are a wide pink halo.

Sarah pinches my nipples. I have not let go of hers although I loosened my grip. Now I tighten them between my thumbs and index fingers again, and we stare in each other's eyes. She draws my nipples away from my body and the feeling is exquisite, so I tug on hers.

"Time to employ the ten-minute rule," Sarah says.

"What's that?"

"Every ten minutes, whether we want to or not, we change positions. Otherwise we might get so stiff that we get stuck. I don't want to release your wonderful nipples, but my knees and my hip are starting to seize up."

Oy! Sarah's so right. As she gingerly dismounts from me, I realize I'm kind of frozen, and have to use my hands to move my left leg closer to the right. As soon as I do, I feel that I really need to lie all the way down and stretch out. Sarah matches my position so that we're face to face.

Sarah inches closer until we're breast to breast, pussy to pussy, and thigh to thigh. She and I take in a gasp of air at the same moment. "Savor this, Lillian. I believe it's your first full-body encounter with a woman's naked body."

"Yes, it is. Gloriously so. But more important, it's my first full-body naked embrace with *you*, Sarah." I exhale in her ear. "You. You. You."

12. A Butch with Benefits

I wake up with my mind blown. It's been a very long time since I greeted the morning naked, wound around the naked back of another human. And in this case the human is a woman, although that doesn't feel as big a deal behind closed doors. After making love in the light of day yesterday, we had spent a lovely afternoon and evening together, talking, eating, and then watching a film on TV called *A Question of Silence* by Marleen Gorris that was one of Sarah's favorites. Even though I loved it and had never seen anything like it, we ended up falling asleep entwined.

I fumble for my cane, slip into my robe, and make a pit stop at the bathroom. Once my teeth and face are clean, I hobble towards the kitchen. It's an odd thing about neuropathy. When it's at its worst, I feel it least. It's an inside-out condition: not a matter of pain, but rather an absence of pain or any other regular feeling in the soles of my feet. And what's worse, in terms of balance, one leg is so much more acute than the other.

I'm desperate to brew my morning pot of tea. When I hear the bathroom door closing, I yell to Sarah, "Take a towel from the closet," but Sarah probably hears nothing with the water running. I fetch a towel, knock on the door, and then toss the towel onto the toilet seat. Back in the kitchen I load the tea items onto the wheeled tray-table. If only I had some fresh bread or croissants to offer Sarah. Just in case she likes yogurt, I add a couple of those, too.

With remarkable speed, Sarah turns up fully dressed, her hair in braids, and her face cracked into a smile. "Put those things down, woman," she says to me, "and give me a cuddle. Last night was kick-ass!"

I abandon the tray-table, grabbing my cane which is looped over it. As she envelops me in a hug, I use one hand around her back to reciprocate. "Did you brush your teeth already?" she asks, and when I nod yes, she cups my chin in her hand and kisses me. Small gentle kisses at first, but soon overrun by a tongue that tickles my gums.

When we pull apart, I offer Sarah tea and yogurt, but Sarah says, "Thanks but no, I want to get back to my room, do my exercises, and go down for eggs before it's too late. After all, I pay for three meals. Want to meet me there?"

"Sure. One question though."

Sarah stops at the door, waiting.

"Are we going to start holding hands and be public and all of that?"

"Not for now," Sarah says. "Not until we've talked more and aren't drunk on sex hormones after a night of fooling around!"

An hour later, huddled together at breakfast, our

excited whispers are interrupted when Elaine stops to ask if she can join us. She's holding a mug and a plate. Oy, just what we don't need: an interruption to our bliss.

"Sure," I say.

"Here's the thing," she says even before her butt touches the chair, "there are rumors and I thought you should know. I'm not one to talk about others, thank God, I just wasn't raised that way. Neither was Richard. It was something we always agreed about, but then really, when you think about it, there wasn't much we didn't always agree on. Do you know that feeling? I think it had more to do with Richard than me, because Richard had the same kind of thing with his brother Hank, although Hank passed away about ten years ago. Hank was only a year younger and Richard always joked that they were more like twins than not. Anyway, I'll keep it short. I just wanted to warn you. People feel they're putting two and two together." She nods with a knowing smile.

"Break down the math for us," Sarah says, "What's the two and what's the other two?"

"Well, I hate to mention it; it must be excruciating to be the objects of gossip. But I guess the first 'two' was the blow-up with your family, Lillian. I mean the whole dining hall heard that one. Didn't seem like she even wanted the grandkids around, and such lovely kids. But why was the baby

Oriental? Was that their kid at all?"

"And the second 'two'?" Sarah prompts, on the edge of losing her patience.

"Well the second 'two' was the word 'homo' being bandied around. No one likes when someone uses a slur, but the others" and here she drops down to an intimate whisper with a toss of her hair towards the rest of the room, "are saying that there's no smoke without fire."

She turns her head, and they follow her gaze. Right across the room sit her buddies Frannie and Mimi, blatantly throwing encouraging smiles her way. So she's flat out on a reconnaissance mission.

"That's so kind of you to give us the whole story straight, as it were," Sarah says, amusing herself, "but actually we do have some things to discuss in private, if you don't mind terribly."

She starts the sentence with an exaggerated politeness, but she finishes it with a stern tone.

Elaine stands up, miffed. "Well excuse me. I was just trying to be helpful." She still holds her coffee and muffin. As decoy props, she never even bothered to lay them on the table. She walks over to her friends with an exaggerated stiff posture.

Alone again with Sarah, I ask her a serious question. "How have I managed to get on the wrong side of so many people in such a short time?"

"It's the nature of the beast here, trust me. Many of us were used to living just with our mates or alone, but suddenly we're in a communal situation we don't really have the tools to handle. My theory is that some people revert to their high school personas. I've managed to more or less keep out of it. I'm lucky to have connected with Hiba, Mia, and Jeanne. I love checking in with an interesting crew each evening for dinner, but I also love having the day to read and write in solitude if I want. By making a few good friends – and Hiba is more than just a friend – she's like a sister to me – I've managed to avoid getting mired down in Manor House politics."

"Elaine has her little gang, too. She and Frannie and Mimi seem like good friends in their own way."

"It's one of the benefits and one of the burdens of moving to a place like this. I personally would rather be somewhere with mixed ages, but I've never found such a facility. And now I think I've got a grip on the right mix between friends and personal space."

"Perhaps that's it. Perhaps I'm just woefully unprepared for an institution. Perhaps I should think twice about selling my house."

"You can think as often as you want, Lillian, but don't forget that your house is in the possession of the brat pack at this time. It's not like you can slip into the quiet of your previous existence."

"And it's not like I can easily get up the damned front steps, at this point. But here's something I don't understand. Why are the people here at Manor House making a big deal? You're open about who you are, right?"

"Yeah, I'm out, I certainly am. But since I've been here, I've been single. It's easier for people to accept a lesbian in the abstract than when she's so obviously mooning over a beautiful woman." Sarah lifts my hand. She looks at the wrinkles, the veins, the age marks, the crepe texture of my soft skin. The intimacy chases away any thoughts of Elaine or my kids.

"There's a lifetime written into these wrinkles," Sarah says in a low voice, "and I'm pissed off that I don't yet know the details."

"What do you want to know?"

"We said we'd do an organ recital, but really, I know very little about your health. I know you have neuropathy – which has something to do with the nerves – and that it makes you limp, but I don't know specifically about you, how it affects you."

"How it affects me? I guess it hit me the hardest about ten years ago. I was driving to, well, funny enough, I was driving to the library…" – I lean forward to kiss my beloved librarian, but stop mid-movement, remembering where we are – "…to return some books. I came to a stop sign and stepped on the brakes, only I didn't step on the brakes. At least the car didn't stop and I actually went right through that stop sign. I was pounding down, on what I thought was the brake pedal, but nothing was happening. A car was coming from the other direction and they were honking and honking. And then I saw that these two little kids were crossing the street, holding hands. I freaked, terrified, although I knew I could steer around them. I picked my knee way up and stepped again and stopped the car on a dime."

"Were the brakes at fault?"

"My mechanic said the brakes were fine, but my doctor said that I was losing the feeling in the soles of my feet. This had been going on for a while, but had worsened gradually. That day, I don't know, my neuropathy jumped the shark and I couldn't feel anything. Apparently I was just pushing on the floor of the car with my foot. I wasn't even on the brake pedal."

"Is there treatment?"

"You can hold things back with exercise and all of that, but no, they can't retard the downward spiral. Most of the time I was okay, but after that experience I decided to give up my car. What a fuckin' blow that was."

"Crap. I can't imagine being without my car. It's my freedom. It's my independence."

"Yeah, rub it in. My accountant, out of the goodness of her heart, did a whole spreadsheet and showed me how much I had been spending on car payments and gas and insurance and maintenance and then showed me how many cab rides that would get me over the year. That was the hugest help, ever. It meant a lot of guilt-free cab rides."

"Don't forget that I have a car here so when I'm going places you want to go, you can come along for free."

You've got to admire the way that Sarah puts things. She lifts up my hand again, forgetting her own admonition that we should keep it cool in public, then turns it over, and kisses the palm. "That's sweet," I say. "And I'm sure I'll take you up on your offer. So what about you? Freda told me about some problem – was it your back?"

"It's my rotator cuff, actually, my shoulder. Tore the damn thing about two years ago."

"Did you have surgery?"

"I've managed to get away without it, although the two surgeons I saw said that I had to have it operated on immediately or I'd lose the use of my right arm. They're full of shit, surgeons, or rather, they're full of surgeries and nothing else. At least while I was trying to figure things out, my doctor gave me a shot of steroids. It was almost instant pain relief – like a miracle. When I told Hiba, she said, Hey, you've joined the Steroid Generation. Apparently, that's a 'thing.'"

"But you seem fine now."

"I found a genius physical therapist and although he just about killed me – because of all the time that had passed before I got to him, he had some catch-up to do – he got me my mobility back, about 80%, and about 70% of my strength. Considering the alternative, I'll take it."

"Anything else I should know about?"

"You're going to discover my false tooth one way or another. Either you're going to see it in one of our bathrooms," and Sarah leans closer and lowers her voice, "or you're going to stick your tongue into the hole when it's out. I take it out to sleep and it soaks in a plastic container with a blue fizzy solution."

"Why didn't you get an implant?"

"No way. The bone had receded and the sinus was in the way and it was going to involve like three surgeries. Lift the sinus; bone graft; then the implant. It was right after Alexandra left me and I wasn't feeling lucky. Didn't want to chance so many procedures. But my dentist insisted this was 21st century dentistry. So give me 20th century, I told her. But that's a bridge and it needs strong teeth on either side which I don't have – they both have big fillings. So I asked her what about the 19th century; what did they do? False teeth. I'll take it, I said. I've never done one, she said. It's never too late to learn new tricks, I said. So she did and I'm satisfied, although it can be embarrassing when I'm staying over with a new woman."

I pull back from her, shocked. "New woman?

I'm like one in a long line of new women?"

"Well, yes, you are. Sort of."

I'm floored. I yank my hand out of hers. "I don't know what to say."

Sarah starts to speak, looking around her. She sees that Elaine and her friends are lingering at the table across the way. "Let's get out of here to have this conversation. Let's take a ride to the river."

I agree. Grabbing my cane, I head for the elevator. "I'll get my sweater and meet you in the front in 15 minutes, okay?" Without waiting for an answer, I hobble into the elevator, shaking and flushed. That casual line was like another slap with a dead fish upside my head. Have I entirely misread the situation? Am I one of a bevy of Sarah's girlfriends? Does she date one after the other or maybe several at the same time? Have I been an old fool?

Inside Freda's apartment, I have a quick pee and a swallow of water, and put on my pink hoody. I'm shivering from the rush of adrenalin, from shock, not from the temperature. I hope I haven't burned essential bridges and made myself vulnerable to the wrong stranger. I don't really have a clue about Sarah's habits in the wild. I know that Freda and Lenny love her, but people change when it comes to romantic connections. And in our cases, our lives have been so completely different that we can't even read the unspoken. Shit. It's like that time I stuck my bad foot into the hot water in the tub at my house without realizing that I was burning myself.

Back in the lobby I see Sarah pacing back and forth outside the front door. I know better than to rush and am careful to use my cane properly. Just then, Emmanuel crosses my path.

"Good morning, Lillian, I hope you are well."

"Thanks, Emmanuel. I'm fine. I'm going out for a ride. I just realized that I haven't been out of here, except for a shopping trip with the van, since I arrived a week ago. That's so crazy."

"I will not detain you, then, but to say," he leans over to whisper, "that the gentleman we were discussing on another occasion is now being helped to find a different location. I hope it does not take a lot of time, because I am anxious to be back with my friends."

"I'm looking forward to that." I stick out my hand and, looking around first, Emmanuel takes it and shakes it with warmth.

"Oh," I remember, "and if you think a letter will be useful, I remind you that I'd be very happy to write one to Mr. Meade"

Emmanuel nods. I have the impression that he cannot imagine what use it would be for a temporary visitor to write a letter to the manager.

In the car, Sarah puts a Nat King Cole CD in her player, which relieves us of having to dive into a difficult discussion while in traffic. She drives to a scenic area on the banks of the river where we settle across from each other at a picnic table.

"I guess I could have phrased that a bit better," Sarah starts. "And I do apologize."

"And we probably should've had some conversations before becoming intimate. Didn't you say that first night we spent together -- that that was the way of lesbians?"

"Well, that's the cliché. And we all know where there's a cliché there's reality. I mean folks are all different and I'm probably not one of the biggest talkers, but it is past time that we learn more about each other's histories. Should I start?"

"Well, it seems to me you already did. When you lumped me in with a throng of others."

"Okay, we'll do ancient history some other time. For now, let's start from after Alexandra left me." Sarah takes a deep breath and then lays her land over mine on the wooden-slatted table. "So, right after she was gone, I was in a state of disbelief . It was the betrayal, the surprise, the fact that she'd abandon me without a glance back after knowing someone else for three weeks."

"Is she still with the horse person?" I had wanted to ask this for a long time.

"Nope, that only lasted about a month or two. Then she tried to come back to me, but all the trust was gone and I told her to piss off. About six months later, she sent me an invite to her goddamned wedding – which I shredded. She actually married a retired lawyer, a man. They spend most of the year at his place in Florida."

"Are you friends again?"

"What can I tell you? She's family. If she ever needed me, I'd be there. And perhaps the opposite is true as well, I'm not sure. But who the hell gets along with their family?"

I picture Michael and the family and nod in agreement.

"I waited more than a year before going on a date. And believe me, my friends kept trying to fix me up. Then I went online with a 'no strings' ad."

"Meaning?"

"Meaning, I wanted to mess around, or as you might say, be intimate, but I didn't want to get into a committed arrangement. You know, what they call 'friends with benefits.'"

"How'd that work out?"

"I got a lot of responses from lonely older women, and they'd tell me they were just looking for fun and someone to do stuff with. But it didn't work that way. One after another, as soon as I met them, they seemed like they really wanted a life partner. I wasn't interested in that – I still felt too raw, too burned – and I was as clear as I could be in expressing that. But it rarely seemed to sink in. It was a drag to feel like I was rejecting people, upsetting these women with their expectations. And worse, several times I got myself into sticky situations I wanted nothing to do with."

"Sticky situations?"

"Yeah, it's called 'lesbian drama' – but hopefully you won't have to learn about that."

"So was it all seniors who replied?"

"No, funny enough, a lot of younger women responded and they were serious. Some of them creeped me out. I guess I wasn't interested in being anyone's Daddy. I did go out with a woman named Leslie, who was in her mid-30s. She was actually butch and she and I became good buddies, even while we were sleeping together. She was really honest: said she always felt awkward and weird in bed, but that maybe she could learn enough from being with me, that she could get out there and be a butch to someone."

I don't know whether to feel jealous or not. "What happened with Leslie?"

"I saw her off and on for about eight months while she kept trying to go out with different women around her age. Funny enough, she did finally find someone, and that someone was butch. Once she met that other woman, we stopped any intimate contact although we're still friends. I see her about once a year and, yes, those two are still together."

"Okay, and, well, were there others?"

"I've been out with a number of other women,

but never more than a few times." She pauses to breathe. For Sarah, this is a lot of talking. "But I haven't been out with anyone else since I met you. Not because I expect or demand anything from you, but because no one else seems even slightly interesting next to you."

"Well, if you like me so much, maybe I can admit that I'm not really clear what you mean when you say that someone is butch. I mean I know it means you're not feminine, but somehow it seems a lot deeper than that. I assume it's some lesbian secret handshake that I haven't been inducted into yet."

"That's a good way of putting it, actually. It's a part of lesbian culture. It used to be that most relationships included a butch and a femme. The butch dressed and walked and acted masculine and the femme did the usual feminine stuff of makeup and stockings and what-not. Today the young people don't necessarily do that whole thing, but in the old days it was a survival technique. Let's say you and I wanted to live together. Well, in the 1920s or 30s, no one would even rent an apartment to two women unless they were sisters. And how would we survive? Women weren't given many decent jobs – just maids and teachers and seamstresses. So one of them would try to 'pass,' while the other…"

"Pass?"

"Yes, be taken for a man. She'd take a man's name – JoJo and Lee were very popular in my day – and she'd bind her breasts with an Ace bandage, you know – flatten them out, and she'd try to get a man's job and a man's salary. So the origins, like so many cultural things, were economic."

"But you were talking about Leslie as butch in sexual terms."

"That's a bit more iffy. With the economic reasons fading, the erotic aspect became a bigger deal. Supposedly a butch is the initiator, the maker of love, and in many cases that would have been true. But there's also this contradictory saying: Butch on the streets; femme in the sheets. Cause sometimes it comes down that way, too."

"And are you a butch or a femme? And what am I?"

"You are not formed by that culture, nor is your sexuality. As for me, I was always very butch, but I lost the energy for all that after Alexandra and I broke up. I got sick of getting my hair cut in a ducktail every three or four weeks as I had done most of my life, so I decided to grow it out for the first time and wear it in braids. I'll tell you the truth…"

My cellphone rings. "It's Michael."

"Take it if you want to. That's okay."

I click the phone. "Hello Michael."

"Mum, we have a crisis on our hands."

13. A Crisis No More

"I'll drive you," Sarah says when she sees the look on my face: half panic, half annoyance. "What's up?"

"Michael said something about Emily leaving him and taking Lee and leaving the older kids. But he was sobbing and I couldn't understand him very well."

When we pull up to the house, Michael is sitting on the bottom step, his face in his hands, crying. My heart's pounding with worry, but at the same time I'm a bit annoyed as well. "My god, my neighbors are probably ready to kill me," I say to Sarah under my breath.

"I guess we should go inside," I say to Michael, looking up at the hated steps with distaste. "Michael, go in and get me the four-pronged cane. It's in the entrance closet." Michael shuffles up the stairs, slouches inside, and comes back out with the cane.

"Sarah, you go on ahead of me please." Sarah is about to contradict me until she sees my face. This is no time for explaining that I prefer not to be holding up people behind me when I'm going up stairs. Grasping the railing with one hand, and leaning on the four-pronged cane with the other, I make it up the steps without humiliating myself too much.

116

Sarah waits for me inside the doorway, while Michael has already gone ahead into the living room. Wheezing a bit, I enter and find him sitting in my Lazy-Z boy chair. I hover until he realizes that he has to relinquish to its rightful owner the perch he has apparently claimed for himself. Jumping up, he says, "Please Mum, sit here."

I'm parched from the combination of drama and exertion. "Get us something to drink, please."

Michael goes into the kitchen. "Water or milk?"

Sarah smiles, shaking her head. "Two glasses of water, please." Oh dear. I can hear him washing out glasses. I don't even want to imagine what the kitchen looks like. The living room is bad enough.

Once he returns and sits down heavily on the couch, I ask him. "Okay, what's going on?"

"Emily has left me."

"What do you mean?"

"She wanted to go to this Bonding Camp for parents and their children adopted from China. It's up in the Lake District and I told her she couldn't go."

"I'm not sure what the problem is. Why do you mind?"

"It's enough she's in a group of women who meet every week for a play-date with their Chinese children. This thing cost $150 for room and board and gas for her friend's car. We argued about it a long time, but I put my foot down. She's barely spoken to me, to any of us, since then. Then this morning I got up and found this note."

I take the piece of paper – the note is written in blue crayon – and read aloud. "Michael, there's a meatloaf in the freezer and fresh bread in the bin. Make salads. Give them cereal with fresh fruit. Do what you want. I'll be at the Bonding Camp."

"Wait, let me understand. When you say she left you, you mean she went away for a weekend? That's why you're crying?"

"She left here against my wishes. She left her children – your grandchildren! – in the lurch."

I wonder for a second if people can still see me gritting my teeth in exasperation. They used to; I used to get a lot of comments, but my jaws are no longer like cut glass. No, my jaws have become jowls over the years. I try to smile but it's not so easy. "And what are you, Michael? Chopped liver? Her children have their father, do they not? That is scarcely in the lurch. And since when does a wife need permission from a husband to do something she thinks would be good for her child? Or for herself for that matter."

"Either this is a partnership and or it isn't. I can't believe you're taking her side, Mum. Really, of all people in the world, I thought you'd support me."

"Michael, I *do* support you, in case you forgot. You're living in my house rent-free, remember?

You're preventing me from doing what *I* want, which is to sell it, remember? I'm giving you money so that the kids have what they need for school, remember?"

Michael nods his head again and again, glum. "I know all that. And I've never figured out a way to thank you for everything." He rubs his eyes, swipes his hands over his face and then looks me straight in the eyes like he hasn't done in a long time. "Just like I never figured out how to ask you properly if we could move in. I'm so sorry we landed on you just when you wanted to put the house on the market. I know now I shouldn't have left a reliable job for a start-up. I know we have more kids than we can afford. Trust me, Mum, I know what a mess I've made of things. But that's all the more reason why I count on Emily. I tell you, if it wasn't for the kids, I wouldn't let her back in."

"Where are the kids, anyway? I'd like to see them before I go."

"They're on an overnight with friends. Emily arranged it earlier in the week."

What? Just when I think Michael is getting a compassionate grip on things, it turns out Emily even set up overnights for the children. I swivel to look at Sarah, but she's dropped her head, probably trying to repress a grin. I don't know whether to laugh or cry.

"Michael, honey, I don't know what's going on

with you and Emily. And I understand this is a tough time for all of you. But maybe being with those other women is an escape for her like all those sports shows on TV are for you."

"That's different. I'm here when I'm watching. And it doesn't cost $150."

"That's fair enough," I say. "That's a lot of money to spend without the two of you agreeing."

Michael looks sullen. I'm sure there's something else. "Do you want to talk about other stuff that's bothering you?" I ask.

"I'm sure you're sick of my moaning, Mum, but I sorta had my heart broken yesterday. I had a job interview on Thursday and I felt like it went really well. Okay, so it's another start-up, but they're doing research into nanotech – which our company was doing as well. This group is working on materials that can detect allergens. Like to eventually make a bracelet or watchband or something that would warn a person that there were peanuts in the room. Something like that. So they need a couple of computer engineers and I thought I did a good job at the interview and that maybe I'd have good news for everyone. But they called me yesterday and said I didn't get it. They said there's too much bad press about my last company right now and their CEO didn't want anyone associated with it."

"Oh Michael," Sarah says, "That's awful. What

bad luck. No wonder you're feeling so down."

He looks at her in surprise. "Well, thanks Sarah." It's the first civil exchange they've had.

"What a disappointment, honey, but maybe the good interview is a sign that things are going to turn around for you soon."

"It doesn't feel that way, Mum."

"I have an idea," Sarah says. "Why don't you come back to Manor House with us and have dinner there.

Again Michael is surprised again. And so am I. He thinks about it. And thinks about it some more.

I pipe up. "That's a great idea, Sarah."

Michael shakes his head. "You know what? I really appreciate the invite, but I don't feel up to meeting new people and all of that. Can I take a raincheck?"

"Of course you can," I say.

I don't know what else to say, so I stand up. "Come walk down the steps with me, Michael. Now I understand why you're feeling abandoned by Emily. Does she know about this disappointment?"

He shakes his head. "I figured I'd tell her over breakfast. I only got the rejection from them last night – an email – while she was bathing the baby. So I never got to tell her yesterday. Then she was gone this morning."

"That's a shame. Life is too often full of overlapping needs conflicting with each other. I can see that Emily is pretty damned obsessed with Lee, and probably isn't paying enough attention to what's going on with you. Once you get a job, things will sort themselves out."

I try to sound upbeat. It's an effort. I struggle out of my comfy chair. Sarah jumps up and heads out the door in front of me. Michael follows me and I use my regular cane to walk down the stairs. I take my time. Sarah's already on the sidewalk looking up. I can hear Michael breathing behind me.

At the car I turn and hold my arms out. My baby boy is sure going through a rough patch, but I have a feeling that he's the only one who can turn it around. We have a fumbled embrace. "Give my love to the kids and to Emily. Tell them I'll come visit again when we can all be together. And try to be generous to Emily since she's going through some of what you're going through."

He starts to object. "*Some*, I said, not all. For sure, not all."

Sarah and Michael mumble goodbyes and we drive off.

"Well that was sad," I say. "Men can be so ridiculous and so poignant at the same time."

"What was Bernard like?"

"Not like Michael, that's for sure. He was like a lot of men of his generation. World War II really defined him. He was in the Military Police, mostly in Brussels. It was the most significant experience of his life, but he never talked about it. And that kind of carried over into everything. He just didn't talk about things. He wasn't really there for me or the boys. If you asked him, he would probably say he was very busy doing his duty. I mean he was a hard worker. He worked full-time while he studied engineering on the GI Bill. Then he got a decent job at a steel mill and after about 20 years he invented some kind of air vent that all the mills wanted and that meant we became pretty comfortable, long after it would do us much good in some ways. He was a nice guy, but later in life he got weirdly self-conscious about a stoop he'd developed. A rounded back."

"So Michael's a bit like Bernard – his back is pretty round as well."

"What can I tell you? I don't really know who Michael takes after. But Norman? Now that's another story. He was so much like my own dad. He was a laugh a minute, always the joker, and sweet as sugar."

"So Norman was your firstborn? Freda told me he was killed in a car accident."

"Bernard bought him a car when he was 17. I always blame the G.I. Bill for his death, because without it Bernard wouldn't have been educated and gotten a job that meant he could afford that fucking car. I was against the car. Norman was very social and always had a gang piled into that car. Three other kids were hurt when that jeep hit Norman's car – one of them was permanently blinded. Only Norman died."

"You never mention him."

"It was a decision Bernard made. He couldn't bear it, he said, and he kind of banished Norman from our lives. The two of us lived in the emotional dark for several years. I guess I got in the habit, but it doesn't mean I don't think of Norman every day of my life. Michael was born later. I think we coddled him, treated him with kid gloves, went everywhere with him, didn't want to let him out of our sight. Oy, am I responsible for his self-absorption?"

"Christ, Lillian. He's a grown man. Got a family of his own. Only *he* is responsible for himself."

"Deep down I agree with that. I really do. It's just that I often worry that his selfishness is our fault."

"Right," Sarah says with false solemnity, "because it is so unusual for a grown man to be self-centered."

We both laugh. "That reminds me of a saying Freda told me when I was whining about my influence on Michael's personality: It's all the carpenter's fault. If he hadn't built the bed I never would've sinned."

Sarah doesn't react. "You know, I have to confess. I love Freda, but half the time I have no idea what she's talking about."

"Maybe you have to be Jewish. I think she's a scream."

We drive in comfortable silence for a while.

"And your sex life with Bernard. Was it hot?"

I'm a bit taken aback. I never really judged it that way. "You know, I don't think I've ever discussed our sex life with anyone. Maybe a bit with my doctor – you know, birth control and all that."

"It's clear you were never in the women's liberation movement, baby." Baby! It's the first time either of us has used that kind of affectionate term – well, outside the bedroom anyway. But Sarah continues. "We dissected our sex lives and shared everything from tips to warnings."

"I can't imagine it."

"Why not?"

"I don't know. Probably because Bernard didn't believe in publicly airing family business."

"Yeah, that's the trick of marriage and the family. That's how people inside families never realize that there are lots of other miserable people stuck in similar situations. That's even how abuse goes on: each family thinks it's only them. In the early days of the women's liberation movement we were amazed at how similar our confessions were. Of course I was much older than most of my friends, but we told the truth about our real lives, our emotions, our sexual feelings, violence that had happened to us but that we had never talked about it before. And the most common reaction was, "You too?!"

"It's not that I think there was anything unique about my life with Bernard. But I did buy into the privacy bit. I guess I missed out."

"Did you and Bernard have fun?"

"Fun? You mean in bed? No, I wouldn't really call it fun. It got better when I read about the clitoris in the early 1970s. Somehow we both had missed that. It took Bernard some years to buy into that, but eventually he did. Well, sometimes."

"Did you have variety? Intimacy?"

"Variety? No, he wasn't having any of that. Well, wait a minute. He did say he was a 'legs man,' so he liked me to wear short nighties and walk back and forth at the foot of the bed while he touched himself. That was about as wild as he got."

"Well, *we* are going to have fun! There's no time to lose. Gotta get in all the sexual fun we can manage."

"I guess I should be embarrassed when you say things like that, but, goddammit, sounds good to me! So would a nap. Just that one trip up and one trip down the stairs at my house were tough, especially as they hadn't been swept. Little twigs and stones and stuff put me off my balance. Anyway, I hope I have time before dinner for an hour's snooze."

At 6:00 the horrid phone siren rings. Sarah asks me, "Are you awake?"

"Yeah, but still in bed after my nap."

"Sorry to disturb you, but I wanted you to know that Jeanne was taken to the hospital with another of her heart incidents while we were out this afternoon. Hiba was with her until the ambulance came and she told me about it. Nancy from the office went with Hiba. So that's the bad news. The good news is that you can have her seat for dinner. If you move your butt and get down here in a quarter of an hour."

"Consider it done. I'm hanging up."

I wash my face and change my shirt and head out. Halfway down the hall I realize that I haven't locked the door behind me. Worse, I've left the keys inside again. I return and grab them. I limp as quickly as possible to the elevator, but when I get downstairs, Sarah and Hiba and Mia are huddling around each other in the lobby seating area. It looks intense, so I hang back. When Sarah notices me, she comes over, her eyes red, her face grey.

"We can't believe it, but Jeanne died at the hospital. She's had several of these little heart events, so we didn't get overly worried. But, this time, damn it, she's gone."

I hug her. "I'm so sorry. And I regret that I didn't have time to get to know her, because I'm sure that I would've loved her too."

Sarah hiccupped back a sob and then pulled gently out of my arms, looking back at Hiba and Mia. "I'll eat elsewhere and let you guys mourn through this together." I run my hand down her wet cheek before she returns to her friends.

I look around the dining room and dread the process of finding a place to sit. Lewanda agrees to load my dinner on a tray so I can just eat in my room. As I lower myself onto the bench just outside the dining hall, she says, "You can go on up to your room. No need to wait. I'll find someone to carry the tray up to you since you can't do it yourself." She nods towards my cane.

This happens to me all the time. I forget that I depend on this cane. I forget how it complicates even the simplest task. When Lewanda sees how my face falls, she says right away. "Never mind. It's not a big deal. We're used to it." I make my annoyingly slow way back to my room.

In ten minutes, a woman I don't know stands smiling with the tray outside my door. I sit down to a meal of cold fish, hardened mashed potatoes, overcooked string beans, and strongly sweetened limeade. For dessert: a syrupy *crème brulée*. What does it say about my life that I eat all of it?

Sarah calls to say that she's spending the evening with Hiba and Mia talking about Jeanne. I settle in with a book of short stories by 19th century

American women writers, which Sarah lent me. As I finish Kate Chopin's "The Awakening," I wonder if I've understood it right. It sure seemed like it was about the price women must pay for sensual delight. Of course, that was then. Now is very much now.

14. The Other Woman

I like the tray idea. Maybe I'll have my breakfast and lunch up here for now, and just eat dinner downstairs. At least for the time being. All these dramas, it's been too much, lousy for my digestion, especially as I'm only visiting at this point. Dinner will be less fraught now that there's room at Sarah's dinner table, albeit for a terribly sad reason.

Maybe I can meet people in better ways than over poor digestion and mastication. I look over the monthly schedule, printed out on bright yellow paper and stuck under our doors. After all, I'll be paying for these classes and entertainments if I move in. Here we go. A pre-lunch chair yoga class in the activity room is being held in 25 minutes. I jump into the old stretchy pants and sweatshirt I used to wear at home for my exercise videotapes before the family moved in.

I leave a lot of time to find the room, which is in a part of Manor House I haven't been to yet. After a few dead ends down the wrong halls, I arrive 10 minutes early. Already there are about a half-dozen people seated facing a young blond woman, maybe in her mid-20s. She smiles inanely, uncomfortably, while the others chat and new participants arrive. At 11:00 she hits a button on her boom box, producing a god-awful whiney sound which in its own country and its own context might be relaxing, but which I find piercing and non-melodic.

"Lean your head very slightly to the right and hold, two, three, four. And now to the left, two, three, four. Look up slowly two, three, four. And lower your head two, three, four. And let's start again. To the right, two, three, four. Be very gentle please."

The music never varies: it's a duet between a small wailing animal and a broken toy flute. The instructor, who doesn't introduce herself despite my being there for the first time, speaks in a high-pitched breathy voice that rivals her music on the annoyance scale. In the 1980s I read an article that has stuck with me ever since. It said that postwar American women's voices rose by an octave to a squeaky high in the 50s and 60s and men's lowered. But with the start of the women's movement, women's voices were tested at lower and lower tones each decade. This girl, though, is like a relic from the old days.

Each movement that this instructor suggests, she prefaces with a warning. Don't do it if it hurts. Don't do it too high. Be careful not to tire yourself. It's as if she's teaching eggshells, not elders. If we totally hold back on our movements, how the hell are we going to improve our health? With each sentence, she lowers the expectations and strips almost all sound from her voice until it is more breathy than audible, with the result that within 15 minutes only one guy and I are awake. If I had a hearing impairment that shut out the noise of the "music," I would've been napping like the others.

Apparently all this yoga class has done for me is a good dose of disorientation. Which way is it to Freda's apartment? Wait, which floor is this exercise room on? I'll make it easy on myself. I'll follow the exit signs and go downstairs to the lobby. I'll pick up my newspaper, and then I'll know how to return to the apartment from there.

I wake up a little from the somnolence of the yoga as I make my way down the hall to the elevator. I must say that walking on thick carpet with my cane is pleasantly silent compared to walking on the wooden floors back home where each step was accompanied by a tap, an unwelcome reminder that I needed help walking. In the elevator, I concoct a plan to invite Sarah over for a little smoke and a viewing of her favorite film, "A Question of Silence," after dinner, all as a run-up to an intimate evening. Perhaps I'll even cook dinner. There's time to pull together a brisket if the van's going to the market. I'll ask at the desk.

But as I lift a newspaper from the pile on the table in the lobby, I see Sarah from the rear talking to a beautiful woman. The woman lays the palm of her hand on Sarah's cheek affectionately. They're in the porched-off alcove, so I can't hear what the woman is saying with such animation. What a looker. She has the face of a woman in her 60s, but the body of a teenager. With her form-fitting dress and patent leather pumps, her body language is drenched in seduction and possession.

And here I am, just a few yards away in my yoga clothes: baggy cotton leggings demoted to workout pants and an oversized sweatshirt that says "World's Best Granny," with faded fuzzy flannel white hair on a cartoon old lady, last year's Chanukah gift from the kids.

I feel the flush of jealousy rush up my neck and I don't know whether to stay or go. I have no right to interrupt Sarah in any conversation, but my brain is flashing in scarlet fireworks of adrenaline as I watch the woman run her finger from Sarah's shoulder, down her arm, and then hook onto Sarah's finger. I can't see Sarah's face to check her reaction to this flirtatious woman, but I know that if she didn't want to be touched, she'd sure as hell say so.

Suddenly I lose my balance, and grab onto the newspaper table to steady myself. It takes me a few seconds to understand that another resident, a woman with a walker, has clipped my cane as she shuffled by me, causing my cane to bounce against the table and onto the floor. I was too busy staring at Sarah and this stranger to notice the walker headed my way. The noise of my cane bouncing off the table draws everyone's attention, including

Sarah and her guest. A pre-teen grabs me. "Oh, we're sorry! Auntie can hardly see and I didn't guide her right."

"I'm fine," I hiss, "please don't fuss. Just give me my fucking cane."

The boy's mouth drops open and then he starts giggling, but at least he retrieves my cane. His aunt is less amused. And here's Sarah.

"What happened?"

"Nothing happened. Someone bumped my cane, that's all."

We stand looking at each other. It's an odd silence. The adrenalin is draining out of me, making me feel pale and unprepared for whatever is coming next.

"That's Alexandra," Sarah says after an uneasy pause. "She turned up out of the blue."

"That's Alexandra?" I'm incredulous. I'd swear I feel my blood pressure rising although I know damned well that it isn't something a person feels. "She's not at all the person I imagined."

"Well, she's particularly dolled up today."

"And why is that?"

"She and her family are visiting the city and it's a kind of touristy day."

"Wow, Manor House is now on the tourist circuit?"

"No need to be upset. Really. It's just a visit for old times' sake."

Where do I go from here? It's not like Sarah and I have had "the" talk. The word "exclusive" has never passed between us. We haven't even said the word "commitment." Do I have any reason to be feeling upset? But then, who needs an excuse for feelings?

I'm unprepared for this situation. I don't know the protocol. I don't know the etiquette. I don't know how to behave. I mumble to Sarah, "Call me when you're free."

I turn – but damn it, I never got the newspaper I came for. Feeling like an ass, I swivel back and take one, fold it and shove it under my armpit and limp away. "Later."

In the elevator I remember that I had wanted to check whether the van was going to the supermarket this morning. But, oh, that had been to get the makings for brisket for an invitation I never had a chance to proffer.

I used to pace a lot. Really fast. It was my way of calming down, working out the nervous energy. But pacing while using a cane, well it just isn't the same. I do it, but with a lot less satisfaction. I'm tapping around the crowded little apartment as too many thoughts fight for the attention of too few brain cells.

If my granddaughter were here, she'd tell me to have chamomile tea. Bernard used to tell me to take a nap when I got agitated. I call Freda and, lucky me, she answers.

"Vy exactly are you upset mit our Sarah? You say she didn't plan, she didn't know. Miss Alexandra turned up mit no warning. Is Sarah a guilty one for that?"

"Alexandra was stroking her cheek and everything!"

"Oy, this I vouldn't vant to see, but vat vas Sarah doing? Vas she stroking back?"

"No, no, nothing like that. I think she kept her hands in her pockets."

"Then for vat the drama? Trust me, *Maideleh*, this Alexandra: Sarah's done mit her. Sarah is a cautious person vhen it comes to vatching her back. This Alexandra lied to her. She is no longer interested in her. It vas a long long time ago. Sarah has been having a good time since then, mit this von and that von. And now you."

"Did you ever see Alexandra? She's young. She's a knockout."

"Listen, my friend. In a beautiful apple, you might find yourself a vorm."

"Freda, seriously, do I need all this at 84? I'm acting like a girl coming to puberty, all hormonal and emotional. Maybe it's better to have seen Alexandra. It's a shot of reality. Who do I think I am, me and my age spots and my gimpy leg and my lumps and my bumps and my sagging and my chins and my trifocals and my, well, inexperience, and my limp tits and my dryness and my maddening family and my forgetfulness and – I'm probably leaving out a whole other list. Compare this to Alexandra and her slender fashion and it all seems like a comedy."

"I'll tell you vat. Bake a cake and then eat it mit Sarah. That's all you need to make everything be sveet again."

"Freda, you're always one with the culinary solutions."

"Vat do the Americans say? The vay to a person's heart is through their digesting."

"Can I ask you something, Freda? Have you ever discussed me with Sarah?"

"Of course, and her mit you."

"Does she care about me?"

"*Maideleh*, honey, you know Lenny and me, ve love you very much. But you, you go and talk to Sarah. I'm too old to be in the middle of all this *mishugas*. You have yourself a chance. Ve're not coming back very soon. Figure it out together."

"You're right. And you're wonderful. Give my love to Lenny."

"And from him to you."

Whatever is wrong with me? I decided when I was 70 that the light at the end of the tunnel was getting brighter and that every day, no, every hour had to be precious. I decided to cut back on the time I fought with the phone company over their bill and with Medicare over their coverage and with Michael over everything. I'm not getting involved with Sarah in order to be petty and jealous. I've got to cut the crap.

I pick the phone back up and call down to the office. "Is there a van going to the supermarket? In a half-hour? Please save me a place." I email Sarah an invitation to brisket dinner and straighten up the room.

15. A Threesome

Tonight was a revelation. A sensual exploration. A sexual explosion. All our senses got stroked. The brisket was tasty, the joint that Sarah brought with her was strong, and our desires were mutual. While she was in the bathroom brushing out her braids and soaking her false tooth, I turned on all the red lights. I really wanted to be able to see everything, but without the glare of white light.

I had decided already that tonight I was going to discover how Sarah liked her loving. When she came into the glowing bedroom from the bathroom, her wavy hair was like a psychedelic halo as the red light lit it up. I gathered up my nerve. I told her in sweet but certain tones, "Don't take over, for once. I made you dinner so I get to set the pace." She smiled in assent as I held her hand and led her to the bed.

I took my time. I played with her breasts in different ways, and could hear in her breathing that she liked best for me to cup them from underneath and squeeze. I traveled down her whole body, keeping my glasses on, and saw in the flesh what I had only ever seen in art. How much more glorious and gorgeous was Sarah's body than any painting or sculpture. And not just her body but my body, our bodies, women's bodies. At 84 I am learning to adore my own physical being through loving, in tangible ways, with my hands and my mouth, the body of my lover.

And I have taken instruction in the power of the Magic Wand to make up for any deficit in my energy or agility. Pressed against my *mons venus* – it's much too strong to apply to my clit directly – it gives me the kind of orgasms that, to my sorrow, I never had before. And it allows me to be generous with Sarah – keeps me from tiring too quickly. Sarah, her Wand, and me: an unbeatable threesome.

16. Culture Wars

Breakfast around Freda's little table is lovely, fueled by the endorphins of an exquisite night, not only the passion, but the cuddling too. We had slept together in easy comfort, not counting the bad shoulder, the numb foot, the missing tooth, and the tension over Alexandra's visit.

"Let's have lunch along the river," Sarah suggests, before returning to her own apartment. "Say, 1:00?"

The plan is short-lived. At 12:45 Sarah calls. "I'm so sorry, but I have to cancel our date. Something's come up."

"Are you okay?"

"Yes. It's nothing like that. Alexandra is in the lobby..."

"Again?"

"She just called me in tears. It seems that she and Lawrence are having a rocky time and she's afraid they're breaking up. His three young adult children are with them on this trip and she says they all ganged up on her. She doesn't know anyone else in town. I'll fill you in later, when I'm back."

"I see. And when are you going to be back?"

"I really have no idea. And I can't talk right now because she's sitting in the lobby sobbing and I want to get down and get her out of there. We don't need to import any additional drama to Manor

141

House."

"Oh, I wouldn't want to hold you up." I know my words are dripping with petulance but I'm unable to dredge up any other feeling, not even sympathy.

"Thanks. I'll call in a few hours, or as soon as I can." Sarah is obviously distracted and her tone feels perfunctory. I understand the situation, I do. But after last night, the timing seems manipulative, as if Alexandra was just waiting to fuck up my amazing mood.

I realize I'm sitting and staring at the phone handset, so I return it to its receiver. All dressed up and nowhere to go. Ready for a lunch date but there's no companion. Who else can I invite to have lunch with me? The problem is that most of my friends are dead, in nursing homes, or have left town to live in a warmer place or nearer their kids and grandkids. My sisters are both long gone. My remaining cousin is in Assisted Living in Michigan. As for Michael and Emily, that would truly be a buzz kill. I'm missing my best friends Freda and Lenny.

Even my book club has broken up because of emigration and death. A woman named Julia is the last member still in the area and still independent. But I don't speak to her. She used to have a kinda hippy view of things – she called herself "spiritual," and liked to brag that her family came over on the

Mayflower. But over the years she changed. Now she's obsessed with fears about other people — other races, actually, whether they're Blacks, Arabs, or, oh boy, Hispanics.

The last time we met up, it was at her condo. It was a number of years ago because I was still driving then. If I had been dependent on the municipal Ride for seniors or on a taxi, it would've been excruciating – not being able to escape when I wanted to.

Funny how I recall the details of that dreadful afternoon. Just a few minutes into the visit Julia, who was about 80, told me that she was working up a stand-up comedy routine for an adult ed course she was taking. "Let me run a few jokes by you," she said. "Everyone else who could listen is dead."

This, I remember thinking, will end in tears. I was reluctant, to say the least, but she didn't wait for an answer.

She fluffed up her grey curls and wrapped a bright pink scarf around her neck, centering herself at the other end of the room. One deep breath and she launched right in. "What did Amos the local Black kid get for his birthday?" I could almost hear her counting to herself: pause, two, three, four. "He got my kid's bike."

I was appalled and reached next to my chair to grab my handbag and my cane. I struggled up from the seat. "Not funny, Julia. Racist jokes are cheap jokes – and not even slightly funny."

"Wait, wait. My mistake. I forgot how sensitive you are about the Blacks."

"The Blacks?"

"You'd rather I said the Afro-Americans? Is that your beef?"

"No, I'm offended that you would smear any group with the general brush of criminality. And African-American people in particular have put up with these nasty generalizations for far too long."

"Okay, okay. Don't leave. Let me try a different joke. Please!" She was frantic, flicking her pink scarf nervously.

Before I could get out of the room, she went on.

"So the Olympics were coming up and Jose, Amos's best friend, was sad. 'What's wrong?' 'My country Mexico is not having a team,' Amos said mournfully. 'Because everyone who knows how to run or jump is now living here in the States.'"

Julia cracked herself up. I already had her door open. "Those aren't jokes, they're insults. There's a reason why we never get together. And this is it."

"Oh, Miss High and Mighty. You think you're better than everyone else with your political correctness."

"You know what, Julia? Fuck you."

Several years later and it still hurts. How could I have sat discussing books with this woman all that time without having any impact on her? There were plenty of hints that she was intolerant – never as pointed as those jokes – but I have to ask myself if I tried hard enough to change her attitudes. I think that I mostly just made snarky comments. I should have taken that course for white people on how to talk to other whites about racism that Lenny attended. Then instead of just storming out of situations, maybe I'd learn how to turn peoples' heads around.

No, Julia isn't someone I want to have lunch with.

All this time as a widow, and I still haven't learned how to go out by myself – not to a meal, not to a film, not to the theatre. For an old person, that's a problem, but it's probably the only thing that's bothered me about being single for so long. I've loved living at my own pace, especially as the neuropathy increasingly defined that pace. I can't stand the feeling that I'm slowing someone else down. Plus, being single relieves me of cooking. A hunk of strong cheddar, Ritz crackers, and organic applesauce makes for a fine meal for me, with dates for dessert or cookies from the bakery. When Bernard was alive, I used to feel like my weekend often disappeared into the kitchen.

I like not having to answer to anyone else's standards. If I leave the dishes undone, if I stay in my nightie all day, if I fart or belch, I'm not bothering anyone else. I can play my favorite Doo

Wop records over and over. And best of all, no bras, no shoes, no makeup, no impression to make.

It's a wonder – no, it's a failure that the women's movement didn't get rid of bras and heels and girdles. Okay, they don't call them girdles anymore, they call them Spanx, but it's the same thing: squishing and squashing a woman's flesh against its better judgement into shapes it would never go on its own. And at the expense of our well-being. I've never been one for stilettos. I kept a pair of basic black pumps and wore them when it was absolutely required – like a work party for Bernard's job. They must be somewhere in the back of my closet back home. My Aunt Estelle made a big impression on me when I was a teenager. Her body had become so acclimated to high heels that she had to wear house-slippers with 3" heels, even when she was just visiting us for a night or two. "My Achilles tendon got very short and threw my hips out of line," Aunt Estelle liked to brag, "because as the kids say, I'm just too sexy for my own good." The result was that she couldn't walk barefoot at all anymore and so she never was able to go to the beach or the swimming pool with her grandchildren.

Ugh. I realize that I've been sitting on this little stool next to the phone since Sarah called to cancel lunch. My goodness, my mind may have traveled to 50 different directions, but my body sure has not. I look for my cane so I can get up, because I'm sure I'm too creaky to just leap to my feet. But first I look at my watch, the one my grandson gave me that's the size of Big Ben, and see that it is 1:45. My goodness. I've been daydreaming for almost an hour! Have they closed the dining room already? I rush downstairs, where the staff are the only folks still eating. I recognize a couple of their faces, so I ask, "May I join you? I was supposed to go out to lunch and my plans got messed up."

They exchange muted but uncomfortable looks. Oh no. I realize I am crossing a boundary that is crystal clear to them – but which I was too full of myself to notice. Of course the staff have no desire – let alone corporate permission – to dine with residents. That's why they're eating after all the elders have gone. Lewanda gets up from her seat. "Why don't I just set a place for you and get you the newspaper?" Without waiting for an answer, she goes to a table across the dining hall and lays out a plate, glass, and silverware. "I'm afraid that only beef stew is still available."

Emmanuel hasn't yet looked up from his plate since I came in and none of the other staff are eating. I've put my foot in it again. I used to be able to feel out a situation, but Manor House is defeating me.

When Lewanda brings me the bowl of stew, I thank her. "I'm so sorry to have disrupted your own meal, Lewanda."

"That's what we're here for," she answers in a low voice.

Of course my appetite has evaporated, but I don't want to make another *faux pas*, so I finish most of the stew and quickly leave the room. Am I one of those privileged liberals who lacks social radar?

Once in the lobby, I pause to read the day's activities, posted on the central bulletin board under the headline "Daily Doings." Alliteration is popular on Manor House signs. The snoozy yoga, an "exercise for the brain" word game, a travel lecture about Easter Island. Nothing there I want.

Emmanuel comes up behind me. "Are you going again to yoga?"

I had told him about how it was more like taking morphine than working out. "No, I don't see anything I want to do."

"I have 20 more minutes for my lunch break and I am going to the garden. Would you come as well?"

We stroll around the path. I complain to Emmanuel. "Are you having trouble getting used to it here? I sure am. I mean, just too many adjustments. I'm living in a building I share with a bunch of strangers. I'm eating food other people are cooking for me. I'm in a new, different kind of relationship. It's a lot."

"Yes," Emmanuel answers. "I feel the same about coming to this country. Always altering what I know. In Kenya, there was no issue about being Black. We were all Black. The white ones were the strangers, the visitors. We had other conflicts – your village, your tribe, even religion, as was the case for my family. But I did not know of racism. I come here and I find that people fear me and dislike me before I even speak. I find that if I don't keep my mouth in a smile, people are scared. I find that if I speak before spoken to in a place where I am not known, as I at first did on the bus, people are hostile."

"Jeez, from majority to discrimination. What a shock that would be. I never thought about that Emmanuel."

"You never had to think about it."

I nod. We smile. He looks at his watch. "My time is over and I must go." We smile again and he leaves me. Alone. Again.

For a moment I think of calling Hiba – Sarah's best friend. She seems like someone I want to know. But I'm not sure of the etiquette: I should probably ask Sarah about that first. At loose ends, I return to the apartment and fall asleep in my clothes on the sofa.

17. New Definitions

It's dark when the damned phone siren rings, waking me up in terror so that I almost fall off the sofa. It takes me a minute to realize that I'm not in bed. I force myself to sit up slowly, turn on the table lamp, grab my cane, and make my way over to the phone.

I'm too late, but I see that it was Sarah and I ring back.

"What are you up to?"

"I was just taking a nap."

"Oh, sorry."

"Nothing to be sorry about. Where are you?"

"I'm in my apartment. But…" and the pause is a long one, "I'm not alone."

"Alexandra?"

"Yes, Alexandra. I'm going to settle her here with a cup of tea and if you're willing, I'll drop by and see you."

"That wouldn't be polite, now would it?

"Please Lillian. It's been a trying day. I could use your support. Let's be the grown-ups we are."

"Oh, so I'm the problem, am I?" I catch myself. Why act like a juvenile? Maybe because the last time I was really into someone I actually *was* a teenager. I take a minute to shake myself out of such pettiness. "Sorry, Sarah. Forget I whined. Yes, do come here when you can. I have no plans so don't worry if it takes you a bit of time."

"I'll be there in a quarter of an hour. Or so."

By the time I change my wrinkled shirt and brush my hair and put on the kettle, Sarah is at the door. I answer it with my arms spread and Sarah falls gratefully into my hug.

"What a mess!"

"Sit down. I'll bring your cup of tea."

"Alexandra's husband has broken it off with her and Alexandra is at a complete loss."

"What's the reason?"

"He accused her of cheating."

"Oh my. And has she cheated?"

"I couldn't quite figure that out."

"You were with her all this time and you still can't tell?"

"I think in her own mind she wasn't cheating, but it's probably just a technicality."

"Meaning?"

"Meaning she's become very close with a neighbor and the two are probably deeply involved emotionally, but maybe they haven't touched genitals. So in Alexandra's mind it doesn't count."

"A woman?"

"Yeah, a woman."

"Alexandra has a pattern, doesn't she? From one to the other, with some overlap to muddy things."

"Yes, she's been with a number of people, but after all she was with me for 25 years – to the day –

and she's been with Lawrence now for a long time. But is length all that's important? I never believed quantity was more important than quality when it comes to relationships."

"Oh." That stops me in my intellectual tracks. "Um, that never occurred to me. I've got to wrap my head around that idea. In our world – me and Bernard – it was always such a big deal how long people were together. It was their 30th or their 40th."

"In the world I came up with, many of our relationships were secret. They weren't public. The lucky ones had a crowd of their own they could celebrate with, but for many people, the two women were totally isolated. I haven't told you Mia's story yet. She and her lover had gotten together when they were both starting out as teachers in an elementary school. As soon as they hooked up, Mia transferred to a different school to teach art, so that they wouldn't slip up. In the 60s they would've lost their jobs if anyone knew. They lived in a semi-rural area about an hour away from each of their schools to avoid running into anyone they knew from work. And they kept to themselves.

"When Mia met her partner, it was her first time in love. She was so excited that she told her family – they were all very close – but they cut her off 100%. Disowned her. Her girlfriend came from a very religious Dominican family who lived in Florida: she told them nothing about her private life and rarely saw them. So there was no family support for this couple. They were effectively sealed off from the world. They had Thanksgiving by themselves. Fourth of July by themselves. But somehow they built a good and loving life."

"I can't imagine that kind of isolation. If I had been stuck so alone with Bernard I would've ended up on Death Row."

Sarah doesn't smile. I realize I sound like I'm making light of this story, although I just meant to make a comment about my married life.

"About a year after they retired, Mia's lover had a massive heart attack at home. Mia informed her lover's religious sister and brother – she thought it was the right thing to do – and they came to town immediately. But once they arrived, they prevented Mia from seeing her girlfriend in the hospital and when she died a couple of days later, they took her body back to their home town and refused to let Mia come to the funeral.

"They didn't have their paperwork in order, so that was pretty sticky. Luckily the house was in Mia's name. She had no one to tell, no one to get sympathy from, no one to cry to. She filled her car's gas tank and just started driving. She hit a big town and saw a church with a rainbow flag. She went in, met the woman minister, and told her everything. Mia's now got a whole new life as a volunteer in that church. She's painted murals on their walls and teaches a children's art class, too."

Sarah stops to take a deep breath. She's been talking uncharacteristically fast.

"Now why did I tell you that whole story?"

"You were talking about quality not quantity, but sounds like those two were together their whole lives."

"Right, right. No, the point I wanted to make was that back in the day, people weren't having the kinds of celebrations you talked about – 20-year anniversary or 30 years. There weren't official rituals like church marriage or civil ceremonies to mark a date. The world didn't embrace a gay relationship no matter how long it lasted or how tight the couple. There was rejection and revulsion. The relationship was tested all day every day. You didn't have a ring or a document to hold you together, and usually no kids either. You just had to decide today, tomorrow, and the day after that, yes, you wanted to be in this twosome."

"That sounds like more of a commitment than a big day in a white gown, that's for sure. But wait, we were talking about Alexandra. Does she want to be with her neighbor instead of Lawrence?"

"I don't know and I don't think it's an issue because the neighbor has no intention whatsoever of leaving her own husband. She's younger. She has several kids. Her husband supports her. Alexandra says the woman doesn't like her husband very much, but she likes the house and the car and the vacations and of course the children. So she's been very clear about not leaving."

"And why have you brought Alexandra home to take care of her after what she did to you? Have you completely forgiven and forgotten?"

"Did you ever hear the term 'main-ex'?"

"X as in the letter X?"

"No, ex as in, we used to be together and now she's my ex-girlfriend."

"Okay, no, never heard of a 'main-ex.'"

I see her tea cup is empty and so is mine. I have Freda's teapot with its crocheted cozy to keep it warm on the rolling table next to me, so I point to her cup as I undress the pot and Sarah passes it to me as she continues.

"It's a lesbian concept. It means that even when there is bitterness and betrayal, usually the two women get it back together. If they've been together a long time, they've become family. Too many of us don't have our families – I mean even before we got old. They've rejected us, been awful to us. So long-time lovers become the ones who know our history, our habits, our deepest darkest secrets. I guess you'd call them our chosen family." She pauses to sip the tea I've handed to her. "How to explain this to you? That even though we haven't been in touch much and even though she stabbed me in the back, Alexandra and I are family. She's

155

my main-ex, the person I was intimate with the longest in my life."

"And me? Am I chopped liver?"

"For god's sake, Lillian. Let's be real. You are, I hope, my new girlfriend. You are the one I'm turned on by. You're the one I want to devour. But just as I will make room in my life for your son and his family, you need to make room for my main-ex. I don't want Alexandra back. I'm no longer attracted to her. But I love her and I will always love her, in that shared-history kind of way. Can you understand that?"

"I can't really. I mean I've had many divorced girlfriends who remarried and they don't exactly bring the first husband along for the ride. I mean the new husband wouldn't allow it. And I know some women who are second or third wives and they complain bitterly about the ghosts of the earlier wives."

"You've got to see the difference. We're talking about two women. We're talking about a sense of isolation, of it's-us-against-the-world – at least for us old-timers. Anyway, it's not about using an ex as a bludgeon. It's about refusing to relinquish the love just because there's no longer a romantic or sexual connection. It's a good thing. It's a creative thing. It's unique to lesbian culture, I suspect."

"Sarah, I didn't even know there was any such thing as 'lesbian culture' until this week, so please be patient. This is all quite new and I'm…"

Sarah's cellphone rings. We both freeze. Sarah says, "Excuse me," and answers. I walk into the kitchen but can still hear Sarah saying, "Enough already Alexandra. Watch television. Read. Write a letter. Do whatever you do, but leave me alone for a little while. I'm with Lillian. Show some respect."

She mumbles a few more words, then closes her phone. "I'm turning off the ringer. She's safe, she's in my place, and I'm now remembering how fucking demanding she can be!"

"Why I think that's the first time I've ever heard you use my favorite word."

"It won't be the last. Now get over here and sit on the couch next to me. Let's neck."

18. Surprise Visitors

The next morning, as I'm picking up a newspaper downstairs, I run into Emmanuel.

"Sorry for sitting myself right down between you and your colleagues at yesterday's lunch. I don't know what I was thinking."

Emmanuel smiles. "It was not a problem. I am not thinking about that. I'm very happy today."

"Why is that?"

"Mr. Smyth is gone. He has moved to Cleveland where he has relatives and where Manor House Company has a similar complex. They let him just trade his place here for a newer place there. I think many people are feeling a relief. And Mr. Meade put me right back on the floor working with the people. So please inform me if you need anything."

"Sounds like Mr. Meade worked out a good solution – good for us, good for Mr. Smyth. Probably not so good for his relatives!"

Emmanuel smiles. "Now that things are settled, I am going to save my money and bring my wife and her sister over here."

"You never told me you were married!"

"You did not ask."

"Oh dear. I'm sorry about that. It's just that we always have so much to talk about – about Kenya. And I wouldn't want to pry."

"Pry?"

"Stick my nose in your business."

"Stick your nose?"

"You know, ask you personal questions. I never thought I should ask you about your personal life."

"I see. Giving respect."

"Exactly."

He thinks for a moment. "I worry about how complex it is to bring them to the States. There is probably a tall pile of paperwork."

"Perhaps I could help you fill out the forms. I'd like to feel useful."

"I have mostly finished. But I am required to provide references. Might I impose on you?"

"It's not an imposition, Emmanuel. It would be my pleasure!"

"Now that I am sure of my job, I am ready to move ahead with the process."

More and more people were arriving for their breakfast, their paper.

"Congratulations, Emmanuel. That is all very good news."

Emmanual nods, looking around. I wish I could shake hands with him or better yet give him a hug, but who wants to stir up more gossip at this point. I just smile and tuck my paper into my armpit.

As I head to the tables, a familiar voice fills the air. Elaine is holding court. "Just the woman I was hoping to see!" she says as I approach. "I assume you heard that Mr. Pushy Christian has been ousted."

"I heard just now that he moved to Cleveland to be near relatives."

"Yes, but you and I know the truth, don't we." Her friends stand around nodding. "We know he was pushed out, didn't have a choice, probably because of all of us speaking up. I'm sure it was us who made it all happen. Richard would be proud of me. One of his favorite sayings was: 'I won't take that lying down.' And we sure put up a good fight, didn't we?" The people around her nod with self-satisfaction.

"I hope he gets on better out there than he did here." No one is listening to me.

"Richard and I had a neighbor once who bothered everyone, you know, a guy like Henry. Not that our neighbor was a Christian. Worse! He was an insurance salesman. Richard always called the guy 'that liar.' How can you tell when he's lying, I asked Richard. He answered: His lips are moving."

I groan. I'm not even sure if I do it out loud or not. Besides the stupid non-joke, I've been standing too long, leaning too heavily on this cane. Neuropathy and standing in one place don't go together. If the legs aren't moving or reclining, they send a weird tingling up my calves.

A new voice adds to the conversation. "Perhaps now that Mr. Smyth is gone, we can have less hostility in the dining hall and create a better feeling." Hiba has come up behind me and is speaking up. She says this with such a warm smile, such a beautiful smile, that people's faces relax and the looks of gleeful revenge fade.

"Yes," Elaine persists, "he was the worst of the worst. Now all the rest of us can be friends."

"That would be wonderful," Hiba says. She has diffused the situation entirely. Elaine leads her crew to their table, with the posture that only needs halos over their head to complete the image of self-satisfaction.

"I'm impressed, Hiba," I whisper to her privately.

"I saw you were in the middle of their unpleasant celebration and thought that maybe I could help."

"Funny enough, I was just thinking of you yesterday, wanting to invite you to visit me for a cup of tea. But I didn't know if I'm 'allowed' to without talking to Sarah." I tried to smile as widely as Hiba does.

"Of course we're allowed to be friends. Is the offer still open? Since Sarah is so busy with Alexandra, we might as well entertain each other. Come to my apartment."

We turn to go but are interrupted by Elaine who has returned. "Hey, I noticed that Sarah has a new friend," she says to me, "And very pretty she is.

They were down here for breakfast."

"Yes, she *is* very attractive."

"Oh, so you've met her?"

"Of course I have. She's an old friend of Sarah's." I keep my voice low.

"Yes," Hiba says, "we all know her. But Lillian, we must be going."

I'm glad to be moving again. "Thanks, Hiba, that's the second time you saved me from Elaine this morning!"

Hiba lives on the top floor in the opposite tower from Freda's flat. As she opens the door, I am immediately struck by the deep reds and blues of the rugs and wall hangings. "How gorgeous!" I say.

"I have surrounded myself with Palestine, I'm afraid. All of these are crafts from my town Ramallah and the villages around it. Every time I go home I buy more and more." I admire the beautiful throws over the back of her sofa and an exquisite embroidered tablecloth covering her dining room table.

"Tea, is it? Will sweet mint tea in the Arabic fashion work for you?"

"Perfect!"

"Sit on the couch while I prepare it."

"May I use your bathroom first?"

"Of course. But wait…" She goes to the closet and gets me a hand towel. It makes me like her even more. I have a "thing" about towels and don't like anyone to use mine or for me to use anyone else's.

When I come out, I settle on the couch. In front of it is a worked brass coffee table, like a very large circular tray with raised edges. "I've never seen anything like this before," I say.

"It's from Morocco," she says. "But I bought it at Pier One in the mall."

She brings a tray with a pewter teapot, thick short glasses, and a plate of *baklawa*. She pours the tea and little shreds of mint swirl in the glasses. "I'm glad I baked yesterday," Hiba says, "or I probably wouldn't have invited you up."

We talk about the various beautiful materials and works of art in her apartment, and through that I learn a lot about Palestine and her feelings about living in the States. "When I retired from my university," she says, "I didn't know if I wanted to stay or return home. But it had been 30 years since I lived there and life had not improved for lesbians." I am surprised by the word coming out in her gentle speaking voice: Sarah had not told me that Hiba was gay. "Life is very hard there now, under siege, and so I took the easier route and stayed here."

Hiba had been a professor of world literature, she tells me. When she came to Manor House, after recovering from a broken hip, she saw Sarah reading all the time. They connected over a shared love of great writing – and over devouring each other's private libraries. From fiction was born this deep friendship.

At one point I realize that I have been sitting here for well over an hour. "Oh, I really ought to get going," I say, standing up. Hiba and I hug at her door and I leave with a greater sense that maybe I can really make a life for myself here in Manor House.

I don't even get lost going back to Freda's apartment. As I'm turning the key in my door, I hear a familiar voice behind me.

"Bubbe!" I twist around to see Lisa beaming, holding little Lee. "Daddy just dropped us off." The teenager immediately catches the confusion on my face. "He said you'd take care of us today. He had to take Leon to his baseball practice."

"Where's your mother?"

"She went to a meditation weekend for mothers. I thought you knew all this."

"No, I don't know any of it."

Lisa is crestfallen. "I thought it was all arranged. Daddy's going to pick us up later, after dinner." Lee leans out of Lisa's embrace me at a dangerous angle, "Bobo! Hole me! I want Bobo." Lee hadn't had much practice on his Yiddish yet, but he tried to imitate the older kids.

"Honey, hold on to Lee until we get inside and I can sit down."

I push inside, and before I've fully lowered my ass on the couch, Lee throws himself on me. I remember how sticky his hands can be, as he crawls up my body by grabbing my clothes. When he gets up to my neck, he buries his snotty nose and saliva-drenched chin in my neck.

Is something wrong with me? Other grandmothers are full of gush and gratitude for every minute they get to spend with the kids. There's no question that I got closer to Lisa and Leon when they moved in with me; but because it was coercive and because it was constant, I always felt resentful. I'm sure I will bond with this littlest one too, but I'd like it to happen within some boundaries, not on the whim of his thoughtless father.

"Lisa, honey, bring me my cell phone from the table over there. I want to call your father and see what the fuck he's up to."

I ring Michael but the call goes directly to his voicemail. I force myself to sound pleasant and ask him to call me. Surely Michael can see through my faked friendliness, but the point is not to scare the kids.

What a relief that at least I can call the office downstairs to sign the kids up for guest lunches. I'd hate to suddenly have to shop and cook. But why should anything be easy?

"I'm afraid it's too late – lunch is in a couple of hours and the cooks are already preparing. You need to give us 24 hours' notice. Sorry."

"Then I won't be there either. But, listen, is there any possibility of including them for dinner? Between you and me, I wish that *I* had had 24 hours' notice that my grandkids were arriving."

"Yes, we found them wandering in the lobby and one of the staff delivered them to your door." There is plenty of implicit criticism in her voice.

"Thank you very much and thank whoever brought them up."

"That would be me. I escorted them myself."

"I'm grateful to you, I really am. Apparently there was some communication hiccup between my son and myself. And dinner? Can we include them tonight?"

"Well, I'll ask Cook to make allowances."

Now what can I do. I ring Sarah – at least she has a car, maybe she'll be willing to drive to a restaurant. She answers immediately with, "Can I call you back in ten minutes? I'm right in the middle of something."

"Sure." Lisa and Lee are unusually quiet and big-eyed, watching me. I'm at a loss, but I also know that I'm the grown-up in the room. What can I do with these kids? There're no toys here, and even if there were, the age disparity is huge. Lisa's 15 and Lee's 2. Either I figure this out quickly, or I'm going to have three miserable people on my hands – them and me.

"Lisa, what should we do?"

"I'm hungry."

"Hungry!" Lee echoes.

"Then how about we get a cab and go out for pancakes."

Lee claps his hands. Spinning on Freda's homemade rag carpet, he sings "Pancakes! Pancakes! Pancakes!

"Lee, honey, this is a building of old people and no one is allowed to scream. Not even me. We're only allowed to whisper. Do you know how to whisper? Wanna learn?"

Lee comes running and flings himself in between my legs on the couch. "Wizder!" he yells.

"Lisa, come help me teach him." We try to make a game out of hissing. Lee mimics us just fine, but when we praise him, he yelps in celebration.

I call down to the desk again and ask for a taxi. "When? As soon as possible." Then I remember that I'm not dressed for going out. I had only prepared to slip downstairs for the newspaper, intending to settle in here for a quiet morning. "No, make that in a half hour."

I find some stationery in Freda's desk drawer – I'll have to replace it – and a couple of ballpoint pens so that Lisa can play with Lee while I change into street clothes, fix my hair, put on walking shoes. Lisa is obviously more accustomed to babysitting her baby brother than she should be. I look up the address of the nearest iHop and write it down. I take up my cane and prepare to be the emcee of this circus.

"Let's go, kids." I herd them out the door and down the hall before remembering that I've left my cellphone on the sideboard inside. "Oh shit!"

Lisa giggles at the swearword and hugs me like in old times. The old times I thought I had managed to flee.

I go back for the phone and lock the door behind me, relieved that Lee hasn't damaged any of Freda's things – at least as far as I can see.

"The taxi will be here momentarily," the woman from the desk says, unsure if she's still feeling critical of me or not. "You can wait right outside."

While we're standing in front of the building, the door opens and out come Sarah and Alexandra.

We three adults freeze. "Lillian!"

"Sarah."

Lisa looks up. "Hi Sarah. Remember me? I'm Lisa. You know, Michael and Emily are my parents. They're always fighting about you and Bubbe."

"Bubbe?"

"It's Grandma in Yiddish, remember?" I remind her.

"Of course I remember you, Lisa. And you too, Lee."

Lisa looks at Alexandra, who is hovering at

Sarah's back. "And who are you?"

"I'm Alexandra, a friend of Sarah's."

Lisa's not very interested in Alexandra.

"We're going for pancakes. Do you want to come?" Lisa is obviously fascinated by Sarah, and wanting to know about this connection between Sarah and me that upsets her parents so much. Between her grey braids, their beautiful jewel clasps, and her mannish clothes, she is one of the most unusual adults Lisa has seen.

Alexandra looks at Sarah, Sarah looks at me, and I start laughing.

"Another time, Lisa," Sarah says, more a promise than a cliché. Lisa looks momentarily disappointed, but then springs at Sarah to hug her before dragging Lee into the back seat of the cab.

19. Emergency

What a relief to finally be relaxing with Sarah. Michael picked up the kids after dinner; Alexandra's husband picked her up around the same time. Sarah and I are exhausted, but alone at last in her apartment. Her tastes are minimalist – everything in neutral colors except the books lining the walls. Everything is also supremely comfortable, with footstools and side tables for every chair.

"I'm not sure this is such a good idea," Sarah says, as she swallows the last bite of her dope brownie.

"Even if it knocks us out, we deserve some laid-back 'us' time." I reach over for her empty plate to pile it on mine on the side table.

"At this stage in our lives," I say, "you'd think our lives would be under control. I imagined that life in senior housing would be calm."

"People are people," Sarah answers. "Jerks are jerks. Feelings are feelings. Your decade doesn't dictate."

"Sounds like a greeting card."

"I think you can see it for yourself, here. All the complications of any extended family." Sarah stands up and lifts the plates from the table next to me. But before she has a firm grip, the plates spill onto the rug, where they bounce once without cracking. She kneels down immediately, but can't seem to get a grasp on the plates.

"Let me help," I start to get up.

"No, stay there." Sarah picks up one of the plates with her left hand, but can't seem to use her right hand to get herself upright again.

"Is it your shoulder?"

"It must be." She breathes for a couple of minutes and then struggles up.

Carrying the dishes, she continues towards the kitchen. "I made lemonade. Want a, a, want a…?" Sarah hesitates, an odd look draping wrinkles on her face. She drops the plates, breaking them this time, and throws out her hand to grasp the door jam. Shaking her head, she mumbles "Weak. Weak." She leans against the wall, disoriented. She slides down onto an ottoman that thankfully is in just the right place. But she is sitting at a crooked angle with her legs splayed open.

I grab my cane and reach her quickly. "What's wrong, Sarah? What's happening?"

Sarah turns her head, but not quite my way, and she mumbles.

"I can't understand you. And you don't look right."

Something is wrong with Sarah's face. Her right eye is drooping. Her mouth opens and closes, as if she's struggling to swallow.

I reach over and take Sarah's right hand. "Can

you hold my hand, honey?"

Finally Sarah looks right at me in a woozy way, but says nothing. Her hand is limp in mine.

"I'm calling downstairs," I say. "Let's get an ambulance."

Sarah doesn't respond. I feel like she's concentrating on remaining upright on the ottoman.

The woman on the desk says she'll bring the emergency team right up to Sarah's room as soon as they arrive. I help Sarah lean her back against the wall and then put her jacket on her, before throwing on mine. When she whispers something, I stop all movement so that I can try to understand. "Mddnss." I don't get it. Sarah looks towards the bathroom. "Mddnss."

Medicines! Medications! I grab an empty plastic bag that's sitting on the kitchen counter, limp fast to the bathroom, and sweep the six bottles that sit on their own shelf into the plastic bag.

I slip Sarah's backpack on over my sweater and hang my crossbody bag over my shoulder.

There is a knock on the door. Two men enter carrying equipment and pushing a gurney. "Sarah's there," I say pointing at her, "She just suddenly slid down when she was walking towards the kitchen. She's not speaking right. She's pale, weak. Her face is funny."

The short white guy kneels in front of Sarah. "Hello. My name is Bradford. That guy there is

Charles. We're the emergency team of paramedics. I need to ask you a couple of questions. Can you smile for me, Sarah?"

She smiles, or least one half of her face does.

"Excellent. Now, can you hold out your arms for me?"

Her left arm rises; the right doesn't.

"This is my last question," Bradford says. "Can you say this sentence for me: I like to walk along the seashore."

Sarah opens and closes her mouth a couple of times before she actually speaks. "Seasheer."

"Pardon me," Charles says to me, "are those her medications that you're holding?"

Flustered, I hand him the bag. He sorts through them, taking notes. "I see she takes a baby aspirin. Do you know if these are all of her drugs?"

"I think they are, but I'm not sure."

"And has she had a stroke or a heart attack before?"

"Not that I know of, but I don't actually know her complete medical history."

"Diabetes?"

"Oh no, I'd know about that if she had it."

Bradford turns to Sarah. "Can we help you onto the gurney to take you to the ambulance?"

"Yez."

The men raise the gurney once she is strapped in, hoist up their own equipment bags, and stand on either end ready to leave the apartment."

"I'm coming in the ambulance," I say.

"Are you a relative?"

"Yes," Sarah hisses.

"A sister?"

"We're a couple," I say. Okay, that hasn't quite been settled yet, but there's no way I'm leaving Sarah to deal with this situation alone.

Both guys look astonished. I guess that they've attended dozens of elders – in Manor House and elsewhere – but we're the first old ladies who ever claimed to be a couple.

"Have you been drinking?" Charles asks Sarah.

"No."

I wonder if the pot brownie is relevant.

"Brown," Sarah says, nodding at me.

"We ate marijuana brownies less than an hour ago," I tell them.

The two EMTs look at each other and then back at me. I can see myself in their gaze: a white-haired 84-year-old woman with a cane who is hooked up with another woman. Surely they didn't hear me right. "You ate what?"

"You heard me."

They don't know how to react. I can imagine what they'll say to the other EMTs when they get back. Lezzies. Stoners. Should I tell them, for fun, that we're pole dancers, too?

"Look, I'm sure all of this seems a bit crazy to

174

you, but let's just take care of Sarah, please. Let's get her to the hospital."

They push the gurney out the door first and I follow, locking it with Sarah's keys. That's when I see Mr. Meade in the hall, right outside Sarah's door. He looks freaked out. I wonder how much he's heard. Or if it's just the emergency that has discombobulated him. I hope he didn't hear that we're doing drugs on the premises. That would not be good.

I don't have time to worry about anything but Sarah.

"Would you like me to get a staff member to accompany you, Sarah?" asks Mr. Meade.

Sarah tilts her head towards me. "I'm going Mr. Meade," I say. "If you'd like, I'll call you as soon as she's seen by a doctor, although who knows when that will be."

"Possible stroke?" one of the EMTs says, "They'll see her fast, at least for an assessment."

"Thank you, Lillian. I'd appreciate that." He hands me his card. "My cell phone number is there on the bottom."

Cell phone! So glad he reminds me. I check that mine is in my bag. It is. And it's more or less charged. I really should pee before we go, but I can't imagine holding Sarah up for that.

They put Sarah in the back of the ambulance with Bradford and suggest that it would be easier for me to ride up front with Charles who is driving. There's no way I can mount the high stairs to the passenger seat. Charles has to get down on his side, come around, and push me up by my butt. At least he remembers to hand me back my cane.

Once at the hospital, Sarah is quickly seen by the triage nurse, who repeats tests that the paramedics had done. The nurse can't get much information from Sarah who, although she's now forming words much better, is still not forming sentences or making much sense. As the nurse reads down the notes of the EMTs, she does a double-take. Looking up at Sarah, she says, "Marijuana brownie? Really? Really?" She's laughing hysterically. "Are you out of your mind? If you were my mother, I'd have you committed."

I bristle. I clench my teeth to avoid saying, "Fuck you." Instead I say, "Well, luckily all around she isn't your mother. She's your patient. When will we be seeing the doctor?"

"And you are?"

"I'm her partner. My name is Lillian."

"Please wait outside in the visitor's lounge."

"No, sorry, but I'm staying with Sarah." I circle around, leaning heavily on my cane, until I'm on Sarah's good side where I can hold her left hand.

"I'm in charge here and I want you outside."

"No!" Sarah makes us both jump with her ferocity. She looks at me and says, "Stay."

I get a grip on my priorities and put some sugar into my voice. "Listen, the last thing I want is to annoy you. But we won't be separated. And we have the right to be together."

"Do you? Which one is the husband and which is the wife?" the nurse sneers.

Sarah's hand tightens in mine. "Just bring us the doctor, thank you so much."

20. Another Unexpected Visitor

After two nights in the hospital, Sarah has been released back to Manor House. She is improving very rapidly, her doctor says, and doesn't need to go to a Rehab center as long as she works closely with the visiting therapists. She's swiftly regaining her ability to speak in sentences, paragraphs even, although individual words elude her. As a librarian more enamored of words than most people are of chocolate, this is a colossal frustration. She can't easily read yet, which is driving her nuts. But worst of all, her right side has not fully bounced back. She has lost some of the mobility and lots of the strength in her right arm and hand. Her face is still a little crooked, but much less so than that horrible night.

Her first full day home, a physical therapist named Ragu visits to assess her. Sarah asks me to be there.

"You'll want to see two other professionals," he tells her, "an occupational therapist this week and a speech therapist next week."

Sarah looks at me, trying to take it in. "Can you explain what these two different people do?" I ask.

"The occupational therapist will work with you" – I'm pleased that Ragu turns back to Sarah to answer – "on daily chores like buttons and zippers and putting on your shoes. And the speech therapist, well that's about talking and writing and swallowing, in case you have that issue." Sarah nods – she's been choking a lot more than usual.

"And reading?" she asks.

"Oh yes, and reading." Ragu works with Sarah on her walking and on building her right arm back up. He gives her a set of exercises she should do a couple of times a day. I'm going to do them with her – it'll do us both good.

Once she's further along, she'll need to go to physical therapy twice a week at the clinic. That's going to take a ton of logistics. I've volunteered to manage the complicated transportation arrangements.

"It's ironic," I tell Freda over the phone one morning when I'm updating her on Sarah's progress. "I'm not used to dealing with ongoing sickness. Most of the people in my life who died did so suddenly or at least very quickly. My parents, one right after the other. Norman in the accident. And Bernard of that heart attack. Other than raising the kids, I've never had to care for someone."

"You vant my recipe for chicken soup?"

"I'm not sure it would have any effect on a stroke victim."

"It vouldn't hoit."

I laugh as she continues. "No, for serious, Lillian, don't let this mess up the romance. Pay a poisen if needs be."

"Yeah, that's good advice. Here's another irony,

Freda. I decided from the very beginning that I would not let Sarah be my caregiver. After all, at 79 she's a bit younger than me – and other than her shoulder, she seemed in super-good health. I wanted to be her paramour, not a burden."

"Para-more. Para-less. Vatever that means, look at you! You got vhat you vanted."

"But now I'm the one who has to take care of her."

"You don't have to. You need to help as much as you think is right. She has got her some friends – her dinner crowd and her old friends. They too can be a part of her team. Don't push them avay."

It's like a lightbulb goes off in my head. Freda's right! "You know, I didn't think of it that way but I think you've just given me the advice I need. I think I've been possessive and staked Sarah's health out as my exclusive territory. And that's a mistake."

"Yes. A mistake. But tell me Bubbeleh, are you two still with the touchy-feely?"

"We're being affectionate, but she wants to sleep alone. Her sleep isn't what it used to be from before the stroke, of course. So I'm missing those cuddles. No big thing. She's improving all the time. Her therapist believes that she won't have much permanent damage. I just hope she herself believes that."

"Ya, I think she knows. I spoke on the phone mit her this morning. She has her a good spirit. She even told me a Jewish joke, lord knows vhere she got it. She said that ven her doctor told her she had a stroke she said she vanted a second opinion. Fine, he says, you're ugly too."

I laugh again, finding it hard to picture Sarah telling a joke like that. Then I notice the time. "Oh, it's 5:30. I've got to go sit with her for dinner. We're eating most meals in her room on trays. She says that until her limbs are working okay and her face settles back, she doesn't want to be out in public."

"Vy not invite Hiba and those vimmen she has been eating so many years mit? They could come too."

"That's a brilliant idea. I'll put it to her. Must run." I make a kissing sound into the phone.

"*Gai gazunt, maideleh.*" Go in health, young lady.

"And to you and Lenny."

I brush my hair, touch up my lipstick, and go to Sarah's room. Emmanuel is there, delivering the trays and talking to Sarah. The two of them have bonded. "Emmanuel doesn't treat me for an invalid," Sarah told me yesterday, slightly skewing her words. "When it's him deliver the food, he treats it like an everyday, uh, job, no, I mean task. Lewanda acts like she's doing me the biggest favor."

"I like Lewanda," I said. "But I think she's

wary. Everyone likes Emmanuel. He's highly educated, handsome, and knows how to talk to people to make them feel special. But Lewanda is older, fatter, and definitely not flirtatious. I imagine people have been rude to her on more than one occasion. Let's not forget her fierce solidarity with Emmanuel when Mr. Smyth was making all that trouble. When I saw that side of her, I realized that she's always a bit defensive around the residents, and probably for good reason."

Emmanuel helps Sarah to the tiny two-seater dining table in the corner of her room, and settles her in her chair. He transfers her dinner from the tray on his cart to her side of the table. He does the same for me.

"I done know if I should tell, but drinking your tea from Lillian." Although English was not his native language, Emmanuel has no trouble understanding Sarah's stroke-affected approximation.

"Oh Sarah. You rat! Emmanuel will think I was passing around his fabulous Kenyan tea to everyone." I turn to Emmanuel. "She's the only one who gets to drink it with me, believe me."

"With a present, you may do what you wish. It is lovely to make a further present with your present."

All three of us smile, Sarah with a crookedness that would be terribly painful to see if I couldn't tell that it is improving every single day. Without being asked, Emmanuel wraps up the garbage bag from Sarah's kitchen and places it on the cart to throw it out. "I'll be back in one hour to pick up the dishes and trays."

With her right hand, Sarah is still squeezing the soft rubber ball given to her by the physical therapist. "You're working that thing half to death, Sarah. Can I put it somewhere for you while we eat?"

Sarah gives it up reluctantly, putting it into one of the many pockets of the workman's apron she's been wearing since the stroke. When I bought a practical, if frilly, apron for myself recently – so useful when one walks with a cane – I picked up a plumber's version for her.

At the end of the meal, I pile up the dishes and go into the bathroom to get Sarah's hairbrush. She undoes the single clasp that I've been using to pull her hair back at the nape of her neck. There's no way I can create her gorgeous braids, so I take the easiest route. This tortoise barrette is big enough to gather Sarah's copious locks.

"It a good thing I don't like wear a bra," Sarah said.

"Because you would need two hands to close the clasp?"

"Yes!"

Someone knocks. I grab my cane and walk over.

It's probably Emmanuel, coming back for the tray. But when I open the door, I'm surprised. Alexandra.

I twist around in Sarah's direction, but she's not paying attention. She's taken up the squeeze ball again.

"Stay there. I'll be right back." I say to Alexandra, closing the door softly.

"Sarah, it's Alexandra. Do you want me to invite her in or should I tell her you'll contact her when you're ready for guests?"

Sarah knits her brow, or rather one brow. She's not ready to see Alexandra. It's a little too early.

"She should not be here. Can you go out and speak to her, tell her, explain her?" Sarah seems quite desperate, vulnerable. "Please?"

I straighten my sweater and nod. "Of course I can. I'm sure she'll understand."

I squeeze out of the door. Alexandra steps back a few steps – she must have been trying to listen at the door.

"How can I help you, Alexandra?"

"I heard about the stroke from, well, let's say from a source, and naturally I took a plane immediately."

"It's a shame you didn't call first. Sarah is just at the beginning of her recovery and she really doesn't want to see anyone."

"Luckily, I'm not just 'anyone.' I'm her main ex. I do hope you know that we spent a good chunk of our lives together." She looks me up and down, which makes me look her over as well. She's wearing a high-fashion pantsuit and expensive jewelry. Her earrings alone are probably worth a year of my Social Security checks.

"Yes, I do know that. And respect that. But right now she's even taking her meals in her own apartment."

"Did you tell her it's me?"

"Of course I did. Trust me, it's nothing personal. But she just doesn't feel up to seeing people and doesn't yet want to be seen."

"I'd like her to tell me that directly."

"This is about as direct as you're going to get." Up to now, I've felt sympathetic to Alexandra, who is obviously rattled by the news of Sarah's stroke. But she is making it clear that the respect and sympathy isn't reciprocated. If she thinks that her wealth and style and composure are going to intimidate me, she's deluded. Sarah and I have been through too much together at this point.

"Alexandra, I just told her you were here. She asked me to tell you she's not seeing folks. I've done that, so if you'll excuse me…"

"I hate to go downstairs and see someone in charge."

"And I hate to disappoint you, but I'm in charge. I'm Sarah's health proxy and, for what it's worth, I'm now her official next of kin. You're her main ex and I do understand that – because Sarah insisted on explaining that to me. From the start. She's always mentioned you and included your times together when talking about her life. But she's not talking that much right now."

Alexandra starts to weep.

I make sure the door is shut – I don't want Sarah overhearing and getting upset. "Let's go to the lounge at the end of the hall," I say, guiding her down the corridor. "There's a private corner with a couple of chairs and it's usually empty."

Using my cane, I lead Alexandra to the window seat. "Sit there." I lower myself into an upholstered chair facing her. Alexandra's dabbing her smeary mascara with an eggshell blue hankie trimmed in lace. What a delicately feminine woman she is. So different from me that it's hard to believe that Sarah could have chosen both of us at different times.

"I'm sorry if I'm being awful," Alexandra says, "but it was such a shock to read about this online, on a lesbian listserv. Funny enough, I hardly ever read the postings anymore, but this time I opened it right away. I tried to call but there wasn't any answer night or day."

"We were probably at the hospital. They kept her there a couple nights. Why don't I give you my cell phone number so that in an emergency, you can reach me?"

Alexandra puts her face in her hands and breaks

down again. "Maybe I shouldn't say this, but I always think, well it's in the back of my mind, I always think that if something should go wrong at home, I can always come back to Sarah. My whole sense of confidence is based on knowing she's waiting for me."

Oy! How do I respond to that? I've never met a person with such an inflated sense of entitlement. "I'm sure she's there for you, as a friend, Alexandra. But Sarah and I, we're together, you know. And neither of us is taking it lightly. Actually, I shouldn't speak for her, but that's my feeling."

"I know. I know. She told me that. But I didn't buy it." She choked a little. "Until now."

I'm anxious to get back to Sarah, who must be wondering what's going on, so I stand up. "I'm so sorry that this all upsets you. As for her sitting around waiting for you, since you're with someone else and have a whole other life, I've been assuming that you'd be happy for Sarah that she found someone."

I could have said it with an edge, but I don't. I say it softly. I do truly find her lack of generosity curious.

Alexandra looks at me sharply, but she can see there's no rancor in my face. "Yes, there's something to that. I assumed that since she was still in love with me when I left her, that she always would be. Really, I never was the slightest bit concerned about any of the women she dated." She pauses. "Before you, that is."

"But why would you be 'concerned' when you're in a committed situation yourself?"

"Because, if you must know, I'm not all that happy with my husband. I miss Sarah. She's the main feature of my own fantasy life. She told me about you, but somehow I was sure I'd remain Number One."

"You are Number One Main Ex, Alexandra. She knows you have her back. The two of you share an amazing history together."

"That's right!"

"But Sarah and I share a future together. And I've got to get back to her. She'll be in touch, I'm sure, as soon as she's ready to see people."

I steady myself with my cane as I stand up.

"Goodbye Lillian. Thank you. But, by the way, don't get too complacent. I'm not giving up so easily."

I shrug and head back to Sarah's room. What a selfish person Alexandra is. So full of herself. Here I behave like Little Miss Goody Two-Shoes, I do everything I can to try to reassure this stranger who wants my lover back, and still she's rude. Fuck her.

I give my private knock on Sarah's door, and use my key. Emmanuel is still there, the angel, and Sarah is asleep. He puts a finger over his lips and signals to follow him into the bedroom. "She was very agitated, so I didn't want to leave her alone. She's been asleep for about 5 or 6 minutes only. Now I must go to my work."

"I hope you won't get in trouble." I whisper as he has.

"I too hope so."

21. Grapes without Water

Sarah's dinner mates are now joining us with their trays around her tiny table. It is a great way for me to get to know Mia and to get even closer with Hiba. Somehow they seamlessly absorb me into their circle. It's clear that when we get back to the dining room, I'll take up the chair that their friend Jeanne used to occupy. The socializing has accelerated Sarah's improving speech, although she still finds herself searching for missing words – and perhaps always will.

When we are alone, we turn it into a kind of word game. "Use your metaphors," was my mantra. One day, on our way to the supermarket in the Manor House van – Sarah doesn't feel ready to drive yet – Sarah is frustrated searching to find the word of the item she had forgotten to write on her list. "Use your metaphors," I say.

"Grapes without water," Sarah says.

I think for a couple of seconds and then, laughing, say, "Raisins?" Sarah throws her arms around me and laughs too. "Bingo!" It is a turning point.

Sarah has managed to turn her physical therapy exercises into a bonding game, by insisting that I do them as well, and by each day adding a few more exercises of her own devising. She looks up everything, researches everything, as one would expect from a librarian; and so she's created a more complete workout regime.

At first her research depressed the hell out of her, but when she discovered two listservs of people who themselves were recovering from strokes, her mood improved. There were many stories of people having low-level strokes, as she had, and of being back to their usual selves, or close to it, within a month. Sarah was determined to be one of those people, so she followed the advice of her new online friends. She began getting out of her apartment – at first just to walk up and down the hall. Once her face had nearly relaxed into its usual look, she resumed eating dinner, but only dinner, in the dining hall. She felt safe with Hiba, Mia, and me. The first meal she drew a lot of veiled attention from people at other tables who were a mixture of curious and sympathetic. Although Sarah seems to have always kept to herself, I think the other residents get a good hit off of her. Anyway, she sits with her back to the room and is cocooned by our group.

Today she feels ready to dispose of her cane, although her doctor objects. She also feels ready to face Alexandra, who has emailed almost daily.

When I told her about my strange conversation with Alexandra, Sarah took it quite lightly. "Yeah, Alexandra is a big believer in insurance policies. She has every imaginable kind of insurance and then supplemental policies to back up the originals. To her I'm like a spare tire, in case things fall flat with her husband. I'm like the $10 bill she tucks into the pocket of each coat. She doesn't actually want me back; she just wants to feel that she's covered, however the dice fall."

I heard no desire, only amusement, in Sarah's voice during this exchange. It boosted my confidence in our own relationship, especially since we've now returned to being sexual with each other. The big challenge has been to find ways to work around Sarah's temporary limitations. Last night was a major breakthrough. I asked Sarah if I could join her in the shower. The hospital had sent her home with a bath chair without ever checking whether or not she had a built-in chair already, which we all have in Manor House. So that gave us each a seat. We both sat in the shower, close together with our legs open wantonly. It was exotic to join the water in caressing each other. Our hair was soaked and our skin was tingling. Sarah's skin was flushed and she was breathing the way she does when she's turned on. I picked up the hand shower. Using a combination of its strong stream of water and my extended fingers, I brought Sarah to an orgasm for the first time since the stroke. It was joyous. It was a massive step forward for us.

In fact, perhaps there's a correlation between that and Sarah's feeling that she's ready to contact

Alexandra.

"I'm going to thank her for trying to visit me and tell her that I'm more myself now. I'll ask how she's doing and end with something like 'Let's stay in touch.' What do you think?"

It takes her about a half hour to type it out. Not only are the fingers on her right hand disobedient, she seems to have to re-learn the whole process of getting her thoughts to the screen. And god forbid this word enthusiast should make a typo – oy!

"That reminds me that I haven't talked to my kids, either." Michael and Emily had both called in the week after Sarah's stroke. I told them what happened and said that I'd be out of touch until Sarah was back on her feet. That didn't stop Michael from texting me two different times to ask if I was free to watch the kids. The first time I reminded him that Sarah wasn't well and was, at this point, dependent on me. The second time I texted him back: "My lover needs me." Predictably he answered: "So do your grandchildren." True to our unfortunate pattern, I wrote back: "Get a job and pay a babysitter." That seemed to do the trick: I haven't heard from him since.

Michael's being so petulant. About ten days before Lisa's birthday, I went online and ordered her a pink computer backpack with a cool design of shiny reflector tape. Lisa was crazy about it and was about to call me right away. Michael told her,

"Bubbe's busy and doesn't want to be disturbed." I know this because Lisa wrote me a thank-you note and included the exchange. A few days ago, Lisa emailed me some photos of herself wearing the backpack. Yesterday I got a little video clip from her. In it she and a girlfriend are walking in the Mall, both wearing the same backpack, but Lisa's is pink and her friend's is lemon yellow. They're looking over their shoulders into the camera, laughing and waving.

"I'm going to go visit my house, to see the kids," I tell Sarah. "Do you want to come? I'll order a taxi. I want Michael to see me spending down his inheritance. It's such an easy way to annoy him."

"Let me think about it," Sarah says. She hasn't been out since the stroke, except for medical appointments and a bit of food shopping with me.

Back at Freda's apartment, I call my house. It seems farther and farther away. Leon answers the phone and the second he hears my voice, he holds the receiver away from his head and screams, "It's Bubbe! It's Bubbe!" Lisa picks up one extension, "Bubbe!!" and Emily picks up the other. "Mother, how are you?" All three of them fight to be heard. I close my eyes and also hold the damned phone-on-steroids away from my head until the noise-makers calm down a little. If the verbal chaos is any indication, I can just imagine what my house must look like at this point.

When there's a break, I quickly speak up. "I'm thinking of coming over either Friday evening or Saturday for lunch to visit." The children are thrilled. Emily says nothing. Lillian can picture her looking around her and thinking, *Oh no, Mother's not going to like what she sees.*

"Not Saturday," Leon says, "I've got basketball."

"And I'm meeting friends at the mall," Lisa says. "Please come Friday night."

"Emily? Does that work for you?"

"I guess so, Mother, but I should check with Michael."

"Has he found a job in the last couple of weeks?"

"No, it's not that."

"What is it then?"

Emily starts to cry on the phone and soon Lisa is sniffling too. "I'm hanging up," Leon says. "I have homework."

"He doesn't always come home, Bubbe," Lisa says.

"Honey, that's not accurate. He just comes home very late, long after you're in bed."

"Where does he go?"

Emily cries louder. "He won't tell us. He says he's working on something, and he'll let us know what it is when he can."

"He's mad all the time, Bubbe. I think he hates

us."

"Lisa, hang up the extension so that I can talk to your grandmother, grown-up talk."

Damn it, I think, I'm closer to Lisa than to Emily and I trust her judgment more, even though she's only 15. But of course I can't contradict Emily in front of her daughter.

"Mother, I don't think he's having an affair. He comes home hungry and distracted. It's just that he's absent. He spends zero time with the kids. Or with me. He comes in after I've got the kids in bed and he wakes up after they're already in school. In between he's on the computer in your sewing room with the door shut."

"We'll figure it all out Friday evening, yes? Would you like me to come after dinner? Say for tea and dessert? I'll bring the dessert. How's 7:30?"

The relief in Emily's voice is potent. She clearly doesn't want to deal with coming up with a suitable meal. "Oh, that's perfect. I'll tell Michael."

I hang up, deflated. I used to be so close to Michael, when he was a teenager, even right through college. My girlfriends complained about their college-aged kids being rebellious or out of touch, but Michael came home most weekends. During that period, Bernard was still very closed and parsimonious with his feelings, so Michael was the person I most relied on.

But since his marriage, it's been ragged between

us. Even before he and Emily were married, Michael told me that he couldn't really confide in me anymore. "Emily's made me promise never to go outside our marriage to talk about what was going on inside of it," he told me. He was embarrassed, I could tell. But that secrecy pact annoyed me and worried me. Abusers, for example, say the same thing. I don't for a minute think that there's any abuse at all in Michael and Emily's home, but I have a sense that she's jealous of our relationship and it doesn't help that she and I never really 'clicked.'

So I'm not convinced that I'll be able to help them sort out whatever it is that is going on, since neither of them tell me much. And now it seems like they aren't really talking to each other either. I know I shouldn't make comparisons, but I'm relieved that from the start Sarah and I have had an understanding that we need to talk things through. Although these are early days in our relationship, we've already faced some heavy drama: the death of her friend Jeanne, the crazed Christian, my own family's hostility towards us, and of course Sarah's stroke. But at least we've handled this stuff together.

I call Sarah. "We're fuckin' lucky to have each other," I say before she can even speak.

"Sounds like you've just talked to Michael? Because I just talked to Alexandra – and I thought the same thing. How lovely to be going out with someone sane. Not out. More in. But you know what I mean."

We laugh. "Come here and cuddle me all night," I say.

"You mean sleep at yours? I haven't done that since the stroke."

"No time like the present. And no present like your time. Come on, give me your whole night."

There's a brief pause before she speaks.

"I'll be there in an hour. I'll make my own way."

22. The Equation

At breakfast the next morning, Sarah and I settle at a table for four – the smallest table available in Manor House's dining room. We're hoping for an intimate meal, but no, my butt is barely in the seat before Elaine comes over to join us. She doesn't ask. She doesn't check. She just sits right down with a huge smile. "How lovely to have you back in the dining room, Sarah. I see you've got a cane now. Catching up with the rest of them, eh? The only time I had to use a cane was after my knee surgery in 2002 – you know, knee replacement. You girls didn't know I was a bionic woman, now did you?" Apparently this is an example of Elaine's idea of humor, because she laughs at full volume until her eyes are watering.

"So I heard it was a stroke. Is that true? What's the prognosis?"

This is the last approach Sarah needs in her first breakfast foray into the dining room. She looks at me, fearing a stumble over her words. I think she wants me to do the talking. I'm not sure, but I go ahead.

"Thanks for your concern, Elaine," I say, searching for a few vaguely relevant clichés that might satisfy her curiosity. "Sarah's on the mend and the prognosis is for full recovery. We're just taking one day at a time."

Sarah keeps her bland smile under control.

"Thank God," I add as an atheist in-joke.

Elaine doesn't get the joke and therefore takes no offense. Instead, she just launches into her usual stream-of-consciousness. "It's hard to trust the doctors, isn't it? I could never trust Richard's doctors. They were always so busy and never talked to each other. So I was always able to spin the situation any way I wanted. I was trying to hide his, well, his deficits so we could stay home together and the easiest people to fool were his doctors. I just spoke for him and laid it out the way I wanted them to see it and they seemed glad I was saving them time, doing their job. Whatever I claimed was fine with them. I made them deal with his physical problems and I hid his forgetfulness. I lost all my respect for physicians once I was in their company so much, I'll tell you."

Sarah's spoon full of scrambled eggs has been hovering, trembling right outside her mouth, since Elaine arrived.

"I'm sure you're right, Elaine," I say, "Meanwhile, you don't mind if we dig in, do you? I hate cold eggs and toast." She nods at Sarah who realizes, oops, that her hand is suspended. But the last thing she wants is to eat in front of other people. Although she looks more or less normal, the side of her mouth isn't yet working all that well and sometimes the food dribbles out.

"So if you don't mind, Elaine..." I nudge again. Am I going to have to get rude?

"Oh! Sorry. Yes, okay, I'll see you soon." She stands and waves ostentatiously, as if to signal to the rest of the dining room that she, and only she, had the inside dope on Sarah and her illness.

We dig into our congealed plates, debriefing about Elaine without saying a word.

"Do you realize that Freda and Lenny are supposed to return in two weeks?" I ask.

"I was thinking about that last night in bed. That we need a plan. There is always my place." She tries to hide her tone of ambivalence.

"You're sweet, but you've gotta be kidding. I mean it would nice to have someone else to blame when my socks go missing, but let's be honest. We can't move in together if we intend our relationship to survive."

"Yes. I just meant temporarily or something."

"There are units open. I just have to sell my house and get here. Time is not our friend."

"Let's try to live long enough to make it happen."

"Wouldn't it be nice to be able to live long without growing old! But as Freda says: 'If you don't want to get old, hang yourself when you're young.' The idea of selling the house and buying a condo here and all of that process is daunting. I don't want to spend our 'honeymoon' phase in such boring frustration."

"I wonder what's going on with your Michael. That's an important part of the, ah, you know, the math thing where one side is like the other side."

"Equation?"

"Bingo."

23. Life is a Cupcake

I had the cab stop on the way at a cupcake bakery to buy a dozen for dessert. Lisa loves them – really who doesn't? Everyone is there around the table, but after we finish the cupcakes, Emily asks the kids to take Lee and leave the adults to talk. Leon is happy to escape, scooping up Lee on the way, but Lisa is furious.

"I'm not leaving," Lisa says. "I'm 15 and I work hard in this family and I want to be part of this conversation. What do you say, Bubbe?"

"Don't stick Bubbe in the middle. Ask your father."

Michael looks at Lisa, who is not pouting. She is determined. For the first time I think that he sees how mature she is. "I don't mind," he says, looking from Lisa to Emily.

"Then I don't either," Emily says.

We all sit in silence for a couple of minutes, until I ask, "So what's going on?"

Michael says: "Well, mother, since you left us like you did, a lot has happened. If you'll all just let me tell it without interrupting me, I think that'll work best. It's a long story."

I top up my cup of decaf coffee and sit back in a dining room table chair that is so very familiar to me – many decades of familiar.

"I couldn't find a job, Mother, not the kind I

had, not with the kind of organizations I knew. I'll spare you the whole saga, all those networking sessions and informational meetings. Nothing. Even though I know there are millions in the same boat since the crash last year, I felt really down. Depressed. You know how I get, kinda paralyzed."

I nod, afraid that if I speak, I'll interrupt his flow.

"I didn't want us to sponge off of you. I knew how disappointed you were in all my wrong decisions. But I'm used to disappointing you. I kept thinking how Norman was so perfect and I was always messing up."

I am shocked. I don't think Michael has mentioned Norman in years, if ever.

"I know I never knew him, but he always lived with us. He was always here. Perfect. Dead. Too young to screw up."

Michael's right. Just because Bernard didn't allow us to talk about Norman doesn't mean the memories weren't hovering all around us. And the pain.

"Anyway, a guy I know who did data input at the same criminal start-up as me is now is working as a blood transport guy. It only pays $12 an hour, not much more than McDonalds. But because he works the night shift, which is 6:00 to 1:00, he makes $15 an hour. He's already a supervisor and said he'd put in a word for me to work as a substitute driver. But I had no idea what it's about or how to drive the kind of van he uses, so for the last couple of weeks, when he's alone in the van, he calls me and I join him on his run. So that's where I've been disappearing to."

"And you couldn't tell your family that?" I ask.

"I was embarrassed. This is a nothing job. I'm a goddamned software engineer, for Christ's sake. And here I am running bloods from a little suburban hospital to the lab that hires the drivers. Not that I was actually employed or making any money. Not that I had a job. I was just shadowing my buddy to figure out enough about the job to get myself hired."

"Gee, Daddy. We wouldn't have worried so much if you had told us."

"Let your dad finish. He doesn't to be want interrupted." I realize that Emily is in on this news, that she and Michael have already discussed it, and I'm glad to see them working together on telling Lisa and me.

"Okay, so let me go on. So I go into the lab office to make out an application yesterday. My buddy met me there, to put in a word for me, but it turned out that their computers were down, so they couldn't process my application. The woman at the desk said that they had fired the company who usually fixed their computers last week, but hadn't yet found a new company.

"So I said I bet I could fix it. She went and got her boss, Delilah, who talked to my buddy and me and then said, "What the hell. See if you can get the system working again." And I did. Afterwards Delilah invited me into her office and I talked her through my engineering history. I convinced her that an in-house expert is better than an outside contractor. And the next thing I know, she's hired me for the IT position. It doesn't pay even a third of what I used to make, but it's a real job, benefits, and all of that. And I'm starting next week."

I'm overjoyed. I want to jump up and hug Michael, but my neuropathy and his neuroses make that a bad plan. This is great on every level: for him, for his family, and – I can't help but thinking – for me and Sarah. Perhaps our dream is closer than we imagined.

"Mother," Emily says, moving us all into the future, "I know you never wanted us here and I know you want to sell the place so I'm wondering. If Michael can get a mortgage now, would you sell it to us?"

"I don't know," I say. "I wish I could just give it to you, but I can't. It's all I have. I'm going to move to Manor House, and they insist I pay in cash."

"We understand. And we're all in this together. Talk to your real estate agent and have her give us the lowest price you can afford, then Michael will go to the bank and see what he can do."

The tension has drained from the room for the first time since they moved in on me. "Call the kids," I say, "let's celebrate with chocolate milk. If this works out, I'll be *kvelling* for a year." Lisa comes around the table and wraps herself around me. "This is fuckin' awesome," she whispers in my ear and we giggle. When it's time to go home, Michael actually escorts me down to the taxi. It is his roundabout way of apologizing for being so impossible for so long. And he's not the only one. I'm going to have to take a long look at my own lack of empathy.

My cab takes me back to Manor House. I call Sarah from the lobby, but she doesn't answer. I leave a message that everything's gonna work out. Then I go upstairs to the apartment and ring up Freda.

"I want you to be the first to know."

"Vat a happy development. He should only get him a morbid from the bank and then all vill vork out. But here's another carrot for the soup. My cousins, bless them, von't hear of our leaving them just yet. In seven veeks is a vedding for their youngest. It's her third vedding in four years and she says no von vants to come. My cousin is insisting Lenny and I stay and make it a happy occasion. But vat she really needs is our help, I am thinking. So you've got another two months at mine. If you vant it."

"Oh Freda! That gives me time to check out the units here and to arrange the whole switch. Dear friend, much as I miss you, this is perfect."

"Von more thing. Mine cousins vant that you and Sarah should come to the vedding. So vat you never met none of them. The more the merrier she says."

"If Sarah is well enough, maybe we'll actually do that. How I'd love to see you." We make kissing sounds at each other through the phone, and hers almost burst my eardrums. Once again I've forgotten to ask her how to turn down the phone speaker. I am in heaven, though, happy for my kids, happy for me.

There is a knock at the door. Sarah comes in carrying a big bag over her shoulder. First she takes out a beautiful bong with a bow from the bag. "I got your message. Let's celebrate. It was meant to be your housewarming gift when you move in to Manor House, but why wait?" And then she pulls out her Magic Wand. With her cane she makes her way over to my CD player and out comes Ella Fitzgerald. She sweeps me up in her arms and begins to nibble my ear.

She pulls back and looks at me. "What?" I ask.

"I was wondering," Sarah says, "if love is blind, why can't I stop staring at you?"

"Oh no, you're turning into Freda with her sayings."

"Hush," she says, insinuating her thigh between my legs. "Let's concentrate on the lesbian two-step."

"Okay, but if you keep pressing like that, I'll have to go and pee."

THE END

THE COVER STORY:
Artists Helping Artists

Sandy Oppenheimer's portrait of her mother is the image on the cover of *Lillian in Love*. As my history with Sandy spans more than 60 years, I have set myself the challenge of portraying our relationship in exactly 100 words:

Sandy is the daughter of Aunt Flo, one of my mother's lifelong girlfriends. When I fled Pittsburgh at 17, Sandy was just a kid. Over the years, when my mother sent me her obligatory, repetitive, weekly letters, she sometimes mentioned Sandy. "Oh dear, poor Aunt Flo. Sandy is living up a tree-house with a hippy." Aunt Flo was telling Sandy parallel stories about me. "Phyllis complains that Sue is doing manual labor despite her degree." I was teaching the martial arts. When Sandy and I finally met as adults, she added a big steaming cup of love to my life.

Sandy has become a brilliant artist with a unique technique. She paints with paper, making collage portraits that are rich and true. And she has repeatedly put her talents to work for me. She created the collage portrait of Sarah Palin for the cover of my book *Thanks But No Thanks*. She posed in all her splendor for the exquisite cover of *Lillian's Last Affair*. Her partner, **John Fisher**, a much-admired marble sculptor of colossal neoclassic works, took that photo. For *Lillian in Love*, Sandy and John offered me numerous ideas, images, and sketches for the cover. And then one day my friend **Judy Schwartz** pointed out Sandy's portrait of my Aunt Flo, a print of which hangs on my wall. Voila! The only thing grander than Sandy's talent is her generosity in letting me put this paper painting of her mother on my book.

If you admire this deeply humane and honest collage of Aunt Flo, check out the rest of Sandy's work and commission a portrait of yourself, your crush, your offspring, your pets, or your favorite author/musician (www.paperpaintbrush.com). And while you're at it, look at John's sculptures and imagine one of them in your yard or the lobby of the office building where you work (www.johnfishersculpture.com.)